Also by Carmen J. Spoonemore

FOR THE COLLECTIVE

DOUBLE

DOUBLE E

BY

CARMEN J. SPOONEMORE

L-TALIA PUBLISHING

Double
Copyright © 2023 by Carmen J. Spoonemore
All rights reserved.

Cover images: *city* © sugabom86; *particle light city* © jamesto-hary via Shutterstock; *face* © Alex Kozlenko via Pixabay

Cover design: Johannes Klein

Book design, cover formatting: Vladimir Verano, Vertvolta Design

Evaluation Editor: Sirah Jarocki
Proofreaders: Omer Hassan, Futuraediting

Print ISBN: 978-1-7369729-1-5

ebook ASIN:

Published in the United States by

L-Talia Publishing, a division of L-Talia LLC
623 West Highland Drive, Seattle, WA, 98119

Contact: Publishing@L-Talia.com

To my Grandfather, I miss you.

Chapter 1

THE HORDE

REGRET IS SOMETHING THAT COMES with time when a person gains a new perspective and can see their mistake. Regret is born of clarity. As Frank Miller sits in the smoky silence of his dingy room, there is no clarity; only tears pooling in his eyes, further distorting the world around him into an incomprehensible blur. The only clarity is this: they will come for him.

As the screaming mob grows closer Frank covers his ears, quieting the shouting voices until they are only a soft, distant buzzing. They will be here soon. Muffled, pounding sounds reverberate from someplace behind him, but Frank is frozen, watching the dusty colorful bottles which line the small window, transfixed by the patterns cast into the room. The roar grows louder and more insistent as more tears fall and soak into his dirty trousers. They can't do anything, he tries to reassure himself; they can't prove that it was him. They can't. He'll tell them that it was the other.

His door bursts open and people cram into the small room. They all watch Frank, unsure if he is the condemned. They stand together, watching him in silence as the horde outside grows louder. But he refuses to look up, choosing instead to watch the glass bottles, which are now falling from their precarious ledge and shattering into hundreds of thin shards. Somehow, it's more beautiful in destruction.

Frank looks up just in time to see a brick hurtling at his face.

Ⅱ Ⅱ

Pain. Blood. The world reappears in flashes, wavering glimpses of what is happening around him. A stretcher, streets lined with hundreds of screaming people, a camera shoved into his face, and the prick of a needle.

Chapter 2

MIST

A FAMILIAR GRAY BUMPY ceiling hazily appears above him. Frank scans the small cavern. Screens hang from the ceiling and a dozen scientists are milling about two large white pods in the middle of the rocky room. A small generator gently hums in the corner. His brain is floating, and his eyes beg to return to sleep. A cold hand reaches around him, pushing him forward. Frank takes a shaky step closer to one of the two white pods in front of him.

"If you are innocent, you have nothing to fear." The words float in his mind like steam from a boiling pot of water. If he is innocent. Innocent of what? Uniting the city? Yes. Even now as he looks into the crowd, there are his friends and his enemies, united in their hatred of him. So, yes, he is guilty. Guilty of finally winning?

Yes.

But they can't know that.

In his muddled thoughts, Frank knows this: they cannot know.

He shakily tries to turn away, but the hands push him closer, roughly attaching wires and a helmet to his head. They lower him into the cold tight pod. The familiar mechanical whirl indicates that the metal lid is closing above him. Frank tries to reach the single small window, but his arms lay limply at his sides.

Blue smoke fills the pod and envelops his senses. This time, icy blue smoke pierces deep into his memories, probing, searching for something. A flicker of motion grows sharper in the blue smoke, and Frank is wrenched forward into the memory.

His hands trace over a chain link fence as red dust collects on his fingerprints. He shifts uncomfortably on the dead grass. He doesn't look up as a teacher begins explaining something serious to them, more focused on the metal fence than his surroundings. He only looks up to see the students joining his class, making the ratty group sitting on the brown grass almost triple in size.

He is wrenched back into the blue mist. The probe lances itself deeper into something he had forgotten.

Frank is tossed out of a door onto the searing asphalt. Hot, dry air floods his nose and the chalky sensation of dust slides across his palms as he rubs them together. In the dark shadow of a tall spine-like tower, Frank sits crumpled on the cracked road looking up to hundreds of windows. Faces peer out to look at him— not with concern, but bemusement.

The probing blue cloud retracts, and Frank floats in darkness before landing on a crowded square platform. His hands tremble from nerves as the platform is slowly lifted by a dozen rattling gears. The smell of the red dust and rubber grows more potent as the platform rises higher. Frank pushes back into the group, squeezing between their legs closer to the middle, wanting to get as far from the open edge as possible.

The blue mist tugs again, softer this time, and Frank drifts into a poorly lit hall with dangling cords and exposed beams. Countless people, all in the same muddled drab uniform, are sorted into two lines. He's tall enough to look over their heads to watch the glittering hologram announce that everyone in his line is being relocated, with the company's "deepest sympathy." Frank chooses to focus on the splotchy concrete floor as across the hall voices shout, yelling at the uncaring projection.

The images flash faster as the probe plunges deeper and deeper into his mind. An emerald-green elevator; a thin, rocky tunnel; trash bags thrown out of windows; a room with beeping computers from all sides; a small thin ledge; cloudlike couches, and his face staring at him in distrust.

The flashes are faster now. They become incomprehensible as the mist fills his mind, finally latching onto its target. His mind spins faster, trying to fight—but the harder he resists, the faster the world spins until he is thrown onto a flimsy plastic chair. Frank squints in the bright iridescent lights swaying above, confused for a moment, but quickly settling into the memory.

As the last traces of blue smoke fade from his vision, only one reality is left: the one where he is lazily reclined on three plastic chairs, staring at the high beams of the lofty white room.

The memory is ripped from his brain and transmitted to the screens in the small room. The white coats watch attentively, hoping to learn whether this is the man who destroyed everything.

Deep in the cavern, the show begins.

Chapter 3

THESE IDIOTS

SOME SAY THAT THE RICH give their money for time, and the poor give their time for money. What they do not realize is that the poor have their time stolen. When time is all you have, it too becomes worthless. These people don't care about his time. And with the same questions over and over—name, age, residence, family, or relatives—they are stealing it.

In front of him stands another intern. This one is slightly shorter and paler than the rest, but they're all the same, tapping away on a small tablet and not giving Frank a glance. She finally looks up and starts going through the same questions as the last three.

"Name?"

"Frank Miller," he sighs.

"Age?"

"48."

"Residence?"

"Grid 238, number B17, OuterCity."

"Family or relatives?"

"None."

For the first time, the bored intern looks at him above the small tablet, "None?"

Frank nods uncomfortably. The intern lightly clicks her tongue and looks back at the tablet. Clearing her throat, she dryly says, "The following section is 'yes' or 'no' responses only. Understand?"

Frank straightens in the white chair. This is new. "Yes."

"Is it okay to lie to protect yourself?"

"Yes." What kind of dumb question was that?

"Is it okay to sacrifice a few to save the many?" she asks in a monotone.

"Yes." Are these supposed to be so simple and idiotic?

"Can we ever fundamentally change?"

"No."

She taps the tablet a final time before robotically saying, "Thank you for your time. Please wait here."

"That's what I've been doing," Frank grumbles. He sinks lower in the thin plastic chair and lazily watches the interns shuffle through the large concrete hall filled with a hundred flimsy chairs. Frank turns to watch the large hands of the projected clock tick past impossibly slowly. He turns away for what seems like hours at a time, only to look back and see depressingly little change. Slowly, very slowly, candidates are weeded out, until only twenty remain.

As the group thins, a common thread appears: the small remaining congregation is filthy, but none of them—including him—seem to care. Stained and fraying shirts contrast with the crisp white of the hall; they stand out like red ink on white paper. The fragile plastic chairs, which used to sit neatly in rows, are now mostly empty and repurposed into footrests, tables, and, in Frank's case, a bed.

"The decision has been postponed. Please wait to be contacted by an intern in the coming days," the authority states. "And please remember to leave your contact information with an intern before you depart."

Frank rolls his eyes. A single intern appears with a tablet near the exit.

A grumble rises from the participants. One asks, "Are you going to tell us what this is for?"

"If you are selected, someone will inform you."

"This is ridiculous," Frank grouches to no one in particular, only to make his grievance known to the world.

The general dissent grows, until the authority finally speaks up. "This is an amazing opportunity for whoever gets chosen. Their life will change forever. So naturally, we want to choose the best person for the job. They will receive the luxury we in the InnerCity have over ..." she pauses, seemingly trying to find the most tactful phrasing, "...you and others in your situation." Pleased with her choice of words, she continues more confidently, "As we make the decision, you all are to return to normal. Don't give us another thought."

That won't be hard for most of these idiots, Frank thinks as he smiles to himself. These idiots, in fact, are simultaneously thinking the same thing. The intern notices each of their controlled expressions momentarily give way to the same smug smile. She turns away from the congregation, smiling to herself. Yes, one of them will undoubtedly be picked.

D D

The train is late again. The volunteers all wait at the same stop, inspecting their new competition. A few trains pass, and the volunteers pause their relentless critiquing to watch the silver bullets streak past.

Of course, the InnerCity trains are on time. Flying through the city on elevated magnetic rails, the trains in the InnerCity run all day, every day, and are always on time. Trains to the OuterCity, however, only run a few times a day.

Deciding he should get comfortable, Frank slides down further into the hard, putrid green shiny seat, closing his eyes for just a moment. One of the hovering lights that illuminate the small platform quietly fades before winking out. As the others continue to judge one another, Frank starts to drift asleep. The silver bullets slice through the night air as they fly through the city, splitting the air and sending it cascading onto the small platform. The cold ruffles Frank's thinning hair and sends a shiver up his spine. The trains spiral around the

InnerCity's towering claws on their floating tracks and reflect back the city's shimmering light. And as they cut deep into the night air, Frank starts to snore.

Chapter 4

SOILED

THE SHRILL SCREECH OF grinding metal rings through the station as one of the many trains abruptly stops. Frank jumps in his small seat, and quickly stands as the others, already in line, poorly conceal their smiles. The silver train waits, humming with excitement, counting down the seconds until it is allowed to jump to life and fly through the city again. The silver doors slide open, and a waft of antiseptic greets them as they file into the train. This is one of the newer trains. It is still sparkling clean, but if it's regularly doing the OuterCity run, it will soon be covered in the red-brown dust that coats everything there.

Soft glowing light emanates from the ceiling as the others push in and sit in the muted blue chairs positioned along one long passage through the middle. A small screen flicks to life on the walls and begins slowly displaying destinations. The small timer is counting down and he is still not onboard. As it counts down from five, Frank pushes one of the other volunteers out of the way and squeezes onto the small threshold as the doors close. The woman he had pushed begins yelling at him but the train, without a moment to spare, launches itself forward into the darkness. Frank looks up to see everyone staring at him. They look away in a singular motion. Everyone quickly sits, not wanting to be thrown by the fast turns. The line of people begins to dwindle, and Frank can finally slide into one of the smooth soft chairs.

The large windows show a flighting image of the InnerCity. Hovering images revolve in mid-air. Buildings are clad in splashes of colors with meaningless words splattered across every surface. It all goes by too fast to distinguish much from the sea of abrasively bright colors. It blurs and becomes hypnotic as the train moves faster through the city.

Frank is jolted back from his trance by a confusing smell of sour tomatoes and cooking meat—the holo-core embedded in the back of the seat in front of him projects a revolving sandwich into his face. Some new restaurant decided to pay 100,000 TUs for passengers to hear and smell their limited-time sandwich, priced at a mere 200 TUs. Frank waves it away. It's not something he could afford, even if it were tempting.

Frank turns back to the window. From deep within the InnerCity, beams of light shoot high above the spinelike towering buildings. Every few weeks, the six beam stations draw power from the city to turn on the lights which transform it into something beautiful. Unimaginably rich colors shine into the city, and the city shines right back. Refracted a million times in reflective windows, the InnerCity transforms itself into a prism, ablaze with brilliant lights.

There is movement everywhere. Everyone from the InnerCity flies through the sky on clear hovering platforms called Zipers. Hundreds of different-sized octagons soar through the city in a dizzying intertwining dance, somehow never colliding with each other or the aerial train tracks. The people are held in place by a thin layer of some polymer atop the disks that glow a gentle blue, securing everything tightly to the Ziper. Their real names have been long forgotten. They are called Zipers because, a second after they pass, a characteristic "zipping" noise follows as the wind shirks and splits into ear-piercing fragments.

Laughter and shouts echoing from the Zipers build into a collective cry of joy as the lights shift and shine even brighter. But for Frank, the sound is muffled by the thick glass of the train window. He leans against its icy surface, watching the Zipers eagerly chase the beams of light. Passing next to the towering buildings, the train is reflected in the shining exterior momentarily, showing a glimpse of themselves. It's all wrong. The perfection of the InnerCity is soiled by them.

As if the train itself had suddenly been reminded of where it was going, it sharply turns, slamming all the passengers into their seats, and heads to the OuterCity. The view translates. At first, only small changes are noticeable in the flashing landscape. Buildings shorten and lights dull. But before long, walls are crumbling, glass is missing from windows, and everything is covered in a thick brown glaze.

This is home.

Chapter 5

MOTHS TO A FLAME

FRANK STEPS OUT OF THE TRAIN and into the darkness. Almost immediately, a cloud of dust billows from the tracks as the train springs away from the raised landing. A metallic flash of silver cuts through the crumbling city as the train rushes to return to the dazzling light of the InnerCity. From here the light looks so unattainable, and yet it calls to him with thousands of unspoken words. Although he would never tell anyone, Frank wants nothing more than to be a part of them. To be important and valuable. To be a part of the better half.

But he is here. All the buildings sag under the weight of time. Even the air itself is somehow decaying. It feels heavy and dry and takes effort for Frank to pull it into his lungs. Some holograms revolve fuzzily, and posters cover the wide light stanchions that dimly illuminate the platform. Layers upon layers of the flyers plaster the poles. Mostly advertising odd jobs and "opportunities," these inefficient peeling announcements plaster the OuterCity. Everything is the same reddish-brown hue as the pervasive dust settles. The cracked asphalt of the platform still radiates warmth as the people slowly disappear into the crumbling streets.

A quiet clanging catches Frank's attention. He turns to look at a young kid kicking pebbles off the platform. Frank had been so wrapped up in his own world that he hadn't noticed the child, who is now watching him. Frank looks away as the kid quickly walks toward him. A gentle tug on his shirt makes him reluctantly look down. A small hand reaches up expectantly.

"No."

The kid doesn't move.

"Beat it, kid," he says, making his unpleasant voice deeper and more imposing.

The kid returns to the small pile of pebbles. Frank pauses for a moment before putting his hand into his pocket and feeling the few coins bumping into one another. Closing his first tightly over the cold coins, Frank muffles their sound before starting the treacherous walk through the OuterCity.

The path home is never quite the same. The OuterCity changes often as buildings crumble and litter builds up along the roads. The smell, however, is always the same. The sourness of decaying garbage festers in the heat of the day and fills every crevice of the OuterCity with its stench. Flies fill the air with a never-ending hum. The result is an ever-thickening layer of non-compostable rubbish that is ground into the many cracks of the asphalt and piled on the edges of roads and beneath the tired buildings.

These streets are the garbage can of the city; none but the residents dare to walk the maze, and only the most desperate scavenge through the mess to pick out any intact pieces of InnerCity trash.

The familiar jostling of boxes in the corner of the dank street makes Frank hold his meager change tighter. Through the gloom, a group of people spot Frank. Recognizing him as one of their own, they look away, returning to their scavenging. Like animals, territorial and protective, they will lash out at any who looks different. Watching the desperate recoil into the shadows, he unconsciously loosens his grip on the coins. Frank's heart eases before stumbling on a discarded box. Like moths to a flame, the greedy eyes of the animals return, summoned by the sudden jangle from his pocket. Frank freezes, contemplating his choices. He grabs the small box he had tripped on.

"Just a headset," Frank says with a forced chuckle, flicking open the lid. No one moves. As the silence grows, so does the tension. They scrutinize him, waiting to see his next move.

"Anything good back there?" he asks the group, kicking the small box that had tripped him, hoping they don't hear his shaking voice. Immediately, the shadows greedily gather their scavenged possessions before re-coiling back into the darkness. Once Frank is sure they have left, he tosses the trash away and continues his way home, although maybe a little faster now.

Fumbling his keys in one hand, Frank opens the door to the kitchen. The thin building looks like it's about to blow over in the ever-present wind, and the corners of the cement stairs have been worn away by time. One of the only free-standing houses, the small shack is on the furthest edge of the city. Small concrete stairs lead to the house where it sits, slightly raised from the street. The flaky red paint is peeling off the walls, and one scraggly bush grows against the stairs. It's old. Older than him. Older than most of the shit in this city, he thinks.

As the door swings, the whole building creaks, and a spider or two falls from the ceiling. Batting them out of his hair, Frank locks the door. He takes a deep breath and immediately starts coughing. The stinging woody powder coats his mouth in a warm glaze. Nothing is protected from the dust that pervades the OuterCity. It's the worst out here, where the crumbling buildings add to the dust that gets blown into the city every night.

Two bolts, three switches, the keypad, and finally, the door jam. A small chime sounds from the ceiling.

"Welcome home. Please confirm identity."

"Frank Miller."

"I'm sorry, I didn't understand. Please confirm identity."

"F r a n k   M i l l e r."

"I'm sorry I didn't understand. Please—," a dirty boot flies through the air and hits the small computer, "—confirm identity."

The second boot quickly follows, and the computer falls silent. Piece of junk, Frank grumbles. The newly scavenged "security system" was, in fact, found in a dumpster. The small box falls from the ceiling and shatters on the ground. Splinters of black and gray plastic litter the ground. Ironic, Frank thinks, as he realizes that he just destroyed the only thing of value in his room.

Kicking the sharp plastic into the corner, Frank stumbles in the dim light over the piles of boxes and crumpled clothing that litter the small room. The house itself is more of a single room with the bed, kitchen, sink, and toilet all just a few feet away from each other. The walls have not been painted since the last owner, who smoked religiously, and the pealing flower wallpaper is still stained with yellow smoke. At least with the dim light it's impossible to see.

Carefully picking his way through the junk on the floor, he makes it to the sink and turns the rusty knobs. The faucet shudders and groans, but only more dust is released. Kicking the exposed pipes just below the faucet, it relents, releasing a small trickle of water. Frank washes the dust from his face. Blasted train always spews that stuff everywhere. Standing up, Frank steps over the small piles of clothing and garbage to reach the one window in the corner of the small house. Glass bottles are stacked in the narrow window obscuring the view.

Squinting through the bottles, and the thick metal grill, Frank peers into the darkness. Nothing. Frank walks back to this bed and lifts the thin peeling mattress to reveal the rusted bed frame and a small black box. He carefully pulls out the small box and unlatches the metal hook. In the wavering light, Frank counts. It doesn't take long. 1,262.39 Thermal Units.

Thermal units, TUs, are the only thing of real value. Countless currencies have sprung up over the years, trying to establish themselves, but the only consistent measurement is the TU. TUs are power; not just monetary—literal power. TUs power every building, streetlight, Ziper, and hologram. Deep under the city, thousands of metal veins pump gas to the surface, keeping the city alive. Life in the city is dependent on this constant, steady flow of energy.

A creation of its location, the city sprung to life after deep natural gas deposits were first discovered centuries ago. Fed by cheap, plentiful power, the city grew and thrived. But the city's blinding lights and insatiable appetite came at a cost. The gas pressure has been sporadic over the past twenty years as the once limitless supply is running dry. As more and more cuts are made, and more people end up on the streets, the InnerCity pretends nothing has changed. Recently, they had to create a physical currency because the OuterCity didn't have enough power to keep the lights on, let alone charge the tablets needed to exchange TUs.

A measly 1,263.78 TUs won't last long. Sighing, Frank puts all the money back into the box and tucks it back under the old mattress.

Chapter 6

I WILL NOT EXPOSE MYSELF

As THE FIRST RAYS OF SUNLIGHT reach the small window, they illuminate the glass jars stacked on the small ledge. As the beams stream through the colored glass, shapes sprawl and dance onto the floor. The colors move up the walls, intertwining, shifting, and shimmering in the early morning light. For those few moments, the world is beautiful, pure, and bright. And then it's gone. Frank sighs, rises from the creaking bed, and turns on the small sink. A small trickle of brown water runs out of the faucet which he splashes, rubbing the grime off his face.

A knock on the door stops him short, and he yells, "Who is it? What do you want?"

Taken aback, the voice nervously calls back, "I was an intern from the volunteer selection yesterday. Is this, uhh, Frank Miller?"

"Yeah…. What do you want?"

"You have been selected, and we need you immediately to begin the program."

Frank raises one eyebrow. "Alright, give me a minute."

Frank smiles. Of course he was picked. For what, he is not sure. But it is good to see they made the right choice. Frank grabs a shirt from the ground and dusts it off. It smells like sweat and dirt, but so does he. Quickly putting it on he grabs his shoes and starts the arduous process to unlock the door. After the familiar series of clicks and snaps, the last lock finally turns, and the door swings open to reveal a small nervous boy, no more than nineteen years old. Frank looks him up and down, amused. This is who they sent? Everything is neatly tucked in; even his socks are symmetrically rolled. Small white circles speckle the navy pants and the burning waft of antiseptic hovers cloud-like around him. Frank straightens, trying to look as professional as possible.

"Your shoes are untied," says the intern, pointing at his frayed dust-caked boots with a gloved hand.

"Sorry," Frank coughs, slowly bending down and fumbling with the stiff laces.

The intern looks around, a small bead of sweat rolling down his neck. Frank enjoys his discomfort—good for them to get a taste of the real world. A small crowd gathers in the street outside to watch. The intern looks around, growing progressively more nervous.

Clearing his throat, the intern asks, "Ready?"

"Yep," says Frank slowly after an overly long pause, lazily standing and stretching. "After you—or are you lost?"

"I am most certainly not lost," the intern says, affronted, before spinning on his heel and marching off into the OuterCity. Frank sighs before following him. You people—so easy to manipulate, he thinks.

Frank breathes heavily, trying to keep up with the intern as he quickly moves from street to street, obviously following his route from earlier. But the longer they walk, the faster he goes, until Frank finally calls, "You want a break or something, kid?"

Through poorly concealed puffing, the intern looks back at him with annoyance. "We are on a time crunch. No breaks."

Frank tries to mask his defeat. "Fine, I just didn't want you to get too tired," he says, before continuing to lug his legs forward.

They must have passed the train station ages ago, but the intern presses on through the narrowing grimy streets. With every sound he jumps and makes a little squeaking noise. A few more minutes pass, and the streets around them start to change. The buildings are growing taller and newer, but the street is growing dirtier. Here, it takes even the fast intern twice as long to traverse the rubbish. Luckily, it is early in the day, so it doesn't smell too bad yet. Frank builds up the courage to ask, "Where are we going, and why are we walking?"

The intern ignores the first question and just answers the latter: "I'm seventeen, so can't fly a Ziper, and I assumed you didn't know how." He turns to look back at Frank, who has decided that his shoes are very interesting. The intern rolls his eyes before continuing with an air of new-found superiority, "Yeah, that's what I thought."

"But why can't we take the train?"

"Take the train? You're joking, right!" He looks back at Frank to see that he was not joking, before sighing and continuing. "I will not expose myself!"

Frank raises one eyebrow

"To germs, infections, and disease!" the kid says quickly, turning pink.

"How the hell is this cleaner than the train?" Frank asks exasperatedly, motioning to the streets around him.

"If you make us late, that will be a demerit on both of us," the intern says, walking faster. Frank, however, stops and waits for him to turn around.

The intern finally notices and spins on his heels before explaining. "Fine, okay—here we are in the InnerCity, a bad, ugly, run-down part of the InnerCity, yes, but it is the InnerCity. On the train, there are all the viruses, infections, and outbreaks you Outers get so often. I will not expose myself to the germs. And look at that … we're here, it wasn't that far!"

He points to a large set of purple glass doors that have been cleared of trash. The intern opens the large door with all his body weight, given it's not much, but the door still swings open, and Frank is waved through. Frank starts walking without meaning to. Us Outers? How could he say something like that? He is not an Outer, he just lives in the OuterCity. Next time, Frank thinks to himself, next time I will set him right.

Chapter 7

HAPPY?

"Hello, welcome to *Next: Medical Procedures and Cosmetic Alterations*. How may I help you today?" says a bored voice from the corner of the impressive waiting room. The walls of the clinic glow with a blue light and angular chairs sit in the corners. The gentle smell of lavender fills the room, and the subtle buzz emanating from the walls is only interrupted by the scraping of a chair or flutter of fabric. It emanates a slow, relaxing energy, but isn't relaxing enough to stop Frank's hand from quivering. He hastily shoves them into his pockets to keep anyone from noticing. But everyone in the waiting room has glazed eyes as they intently watch their BlueScreens. In the front of the room the bored attendant, still not looking up, passively watches a glowing table. The intern clears his throat, and the attendant looks up in annoyance. Her face quickly changes to excitement.

"Yes, yes, my apologies, someone will be with you momentarily," she says, quickly typing into the wide table. "Can I offer you two tea or water?"

"No, thank you," the intern responds tersely.

"We will be ready in a moment, please take a seat," she says with a newfound burst of energy. The intern nods and sits in a set of chairs. Frank follows, annoyed.

"I wanted water," Frank grunts.

"You can't have any water."

"Why not?"

"Because I said so."

"Because I said so," Frank says mockingly. "Screw you, man."

"It's for your own good."

"Ah, thank you," Frank says sarcastically. The intern rolls his eyes.

"Right this way, please," says the attendant. The intern gets up and looks back.

"Coming?"

"What, was he talking to us?"

"Yes," sighs the intern.

"Oh," Frank tries to suppress his surprise. Waits in the OuterCity are never this short, and it often takes several hours to convince someone in any medical clinic that something is wrong; even then, most leave with a bandage or an appointment for several months away, not to mention thousands of TUs in debt. Here, however, they pass room after room, all empty. They walk through the winding complex of examination rooms and offices until the attendant leaves them in an empty room. The beige walls match the chairs, table, cabinets, and medical bed—everything is the same as the countless other rooms they passed.

"Why did we have to come all the way to this room when we could have just gone to the first empty one?" Frank asks.

"Because of this." The intern walks over to the large cabinets in the corner of the room. Flinging the doors open with a triumphant flourish, a steep, dark tunnel is revealed. The sinister tunnel is so deep that it turns into blackness before reaching anything.

"Nope, no way, absolutely not," says Frank.

"Come on, it's not that bad."

"What do you not understand about 'No'? Why can't I stay up here?"

"It's just how it has to be!"

"Why! You saw those people. They won't notice if we start doing jumping jacks on the couch."

"I don't make the decisions, okay? This is just how it has to go. No one can interfere."

"Interfere with what?" Frank asks pointedly. The intern shifts uncomfortably and turns even paler than before.

"Look, I was down here the other day. It's cleaner than the OuterCity, for sure." The intern pauses, and quickly corrects himself, something he didn't bother to do when they were in the street. "Look, I just mean you'll be fine."

Still apprehensive, Frank peers down the dark tunnel and shakes his head again.

"If it's fine, then why are you putting those back on?" Frank asks, mustering some courage. Looking down at his hands, the intern realizes he was unconsciously putting the gloves he wore in the OuterCity back on in preparation for going down the tunnel.

"I have a thing with germs—but fine, if it'll make you shut up." He shoves the gloves back into his pocket. "Happy?"

With sarcasm dripping from his voice, Frank says, "Yeah, actually! After you!" and motions to the mouth of the dark tunnel. The intern rolls his eyes before starting the descent down into the bowels of the city.

Chapter 8

EASIER TO DISPOSE OF

WATER SLOWLY DRIPS FROM the ceiling as their feet squelch in the damp tunnel. The small lights are poorly spaced down the tunnel, so some sections are in complete darkness, and others are blinding. The intern secretly slips his gloves back on and covers his nose with his shirt to stop the wet, sticky air from getting caught in his throat. Frank doesn't waste a thought on the smell or state of the tunnel; instead, he's worrying about the end. What had he signed up for? After a particularly dark and damp section, a dim light marks the end of their trek. As they near the end, Frank tries to look over the intern's head to see an approaching room, but the rock is too low, and he is forced to duck back down. Finally, the two enter a cavernous room carved into the rock. Wires tangle like snakes on the floor, and rows of state-of-the-art computers sit stacked on long gray desks that fit neatly in rows. This must be some kind of control room. The intern motions for Frank to stay put and disappears down one of the many tunnels jutting off the main room.

Frank stands alone in the gaping room. He waits for a while, but eventually his curiosity gets the better of him and he starts to circle the room. Careful to not tangle his feet in the mess of wires and boxes, Frank looks at the walls. Each is covered with screens and diagrams. For the few Frank can decipher, he can tell there is something about the replication of cells and a video game someone had been playing on the computer in the corner of the room. Good to see they're focused. A sound from up one of the connecting tunnels makes him jump, and he returns to where he was standing before. From the tunnel comes one of the interns who had taken down his information in the volunteer hall. She carries a large stack of papers almost as tall as her torso.

"We need you to sign these," she says matter-of-factly. She gingerly sets them on one of the long, gray tables.

"What are they for?" Frank asks, flipping through the massive stack.

"It's so you can get the promised money that is included with this program," she says as if he should already know that. She hands him a red pen.

"Why is it all paper?"

"Easier to dispose of."

Frank takes a chunk of the papers and sits on the floor to read them.

"Oh, you don't actually have to read them; it's basically saying if anything happens, it's not our fault, and with the bank, it's attaching your name and signature to the account."

"Oh, alright." Frank again thumbs through the pile, signing the sections marked with tiny red clips.

"Perfect. Someone will be with you in a moment," says the intern, before disappearing back up one of the hallways. This time, not daring to look around the room, Frank waits, knowing that here "in a moment" isn't, in fact, three hours, but concerningly fast. Just as promised, a horde of people enter the room, all excitedly talking to one another until they see Frank and promptly quiet one another with excited hushes.

"Hello, Frank, it is nice to meet you," says a tall woman from the front of the crowd.

"Uh, thanks, I guess, and who are you?" he says, studying her long crooked nose, tightly sliced gray hair, and white lab coat.

"That's not important. What is important is you—and more specifically, what makes you, you!" she says, pulling a clipboard from somewhere in the crowd of people.

"What?" Frank says, after a moment of trying to decipher her meaning.

"Follow me, Frank."

"Do I get to find out what I'm here for? Because this doesn't seem entirely safe."

"You signed the forms, right?" says the woman.

"Yes."

"You'll be fine."

"Hold on one minute—" Frank begins to say, but the crowd is already dispersing and heading to the rows of desks.

"Walk with me, Frank."

Begrudgingly, Frank shrugs and follows the woman as she begins to walk down the left hall.

"How does it feel?"

"How does what feel?" says Frank, skeptically.

She stops and turns to face him, allowing Frank to catch up. "How does it feel to be on the side of history?" Her voice is quiet, controlled, as if she has been planning this for decades—and, by her age, that could be the case.

"It would feel a lot better if I knew what side I was on."

The woman sighs before saying, "That's the trouble, isn't it? You never know what side you'll end up on. Good versus bad, right versus wrong … even the most perfect person does a little bad, just like how even the worst actions can be right in the end. While I can't tell you what's happening, I can tell you that we are on the side of progress, the side of science. If you do as we say, you will stay on that side. Because when everything is said and done, what is nobler than pursuing progress for all humanity?"

"But how do you know that this, whatever it is, will make any difference?"

"I know that, if nothing else, this will make an interesting experiment. And in the best-case scenario, it might unite the city," she finishes.

Frank scoffs disbelievingly. "Unite the city? You better be performing a miracle or something then."

"Not quite," she says, smiling.

The woman turns to the left and suddenly they enter a medium-sized bright white room with a table hovering in the middle. Long mechanical arms protrude from the sides. He squints in the light and shuffles into the cold fresh room. The oblong table has the same soft glowing light as the walls, but with a thin metal band wrapping along its edge. The metal arms, each with different attachments, are painted white, with thick black numbers along the sides.

"Lay down there for me," she says, gesturing towards the table.

"Why?"

"We need some scans before we can continue."

"Continue with what?"

"The process," she says again as if he should know. That's getting really annoying. Not wanting to feel dumb, and remembering that he needs the TUs anyway, Frank lays down on the table. It's surprisingly warm and comforting. A rectangular arm descends, and the three small, green lights begin to blink rhythmically. As the lights blink, a gentle hum rises, and Frank drifts into sleep.

Chapter 9

PICK ONE

THE BLURRY SURROUNDINGS softly fuse together as Frank slightly opens his eyes. Looking around, he sees a new room, but he is still on the table. He jumps as he sees himself still asleep, going to rub his head, which seems to have stopped working, but his hand is met with a hard metal helmet. Deciding that he must still be asleep, he lays back on the table, and all becomes dark again.

◫ ◫

The first thing he sees is several faces peering over him.

"Oh, oh, he's awake," exclaims one excitedly, moving out of his field of view.

The same woman from before appears above him looking down.

"Have a nice nap?" she inquires. The others chuckle. "We're almost done. We just need you awake for this, alright?"

Frank nods, and the room turns to chaos as excited people rush to find headsets and detangle wires. Heart monitors and IVs are plugged into Frank as he sits still, still not entirely sure what's happening.

"Everything feel good?" she asks.

"I guess. You're still not going to tell me what this is for, are you?"

She smiles and walks back out of his line of vision. Muffled voices rise from behind him, "Turning on in 3...2... it's on."

Nothing seems to be happening, but the ordinarily talkative interns are surprisingly quiet. The quietness, the bright lights, the sweat pooling under the heavy helmet... Why isn't anything happening? The quiet. The lights. The heavy, heavy helmet. Why is nothing changing? Quiet. Dimming. Heavy, heavy. Quiet. Heavy. Quiet. Heavy. Heavy. Heavy. Lights. Sound. The soft lights glow gently and the whirling ceases.

"How was that?"

"Fine," Frank says, confused.

"Good. Sit up, please."

He does and is presented with two TU coins, a 10 and a 25.

"Pick one."

"Is this a joke?" he says, looking at the white coat and, after she doesn't react, to the other dozen people standing tightly packed in the lightly humming room.

"Just do it." He takes the 25, obviously.

Next, two gum wrappers are placed onto the tray. In bright blue one screams, "New! Yummy Kick Zappers!" In green, the other announces, "New! Tasty Sugar Blasters!"

"Seriously? These are for kids." Everyone waits.

"Oh, I get it, this is still the—okay, whatever," Frank grumbles, grabbing the blue wrapper.

The group in the back furiously taps on tablets.

"Okay, now will you please follow me?"

Frank gets up and follows an intern down the rocky carved hall to a shining metallic door. As the intern opens the door to let him in, the other door opens simultaneously, revealing ... himself.

Frank walks into the room, wondering why a mirror spans the room's length, and sits down at the small table. It seamlessly meets the smooth gray walls. He looks at his reflection. It seems almost too real; it must be the newest advancement in the InnerCity. But still, it makes him want to reach out and touch his reflection. He does, and as he reaches his arm up, he watches his mirror image do the same, reaching out. Huh, it must be broken—it's raising the wrong arm. He touches the shoulder of the reflection. It's warm. The two quickly recoil and jump out of their chairs and stare at each other.

"Are you?" they say simultaneously.

"Are we?" they both say again.

"How? Okay, this is getting annoying. Stop. You stop. Me first. No. I'll talk, then you," they say simultaneously.

They stare at each other exasperatedly. The third door opens, and the Franks look at each other.

"Not another," they both say, turning to look at the door.

"No, there's just two of you," says the same scientist from before.

"Are you going to tell us exactly what happened?" they both say again, looking at each other.

"I think you've already figured that out, haven't you?"

"You copied me. No, they copied me. No, me."

Cutting the two of them off, she proudly says, "You are both copies of the other: same memories, same thoughts, same body. A perfect double."

The Franks turn from her to look at each other again. Trying to test the other, they both put their arms up. Seeing the other had done the same, they both start hopping on their left foot, then waving and dancing.

"Okay, I believe you," they say, simultaneously.

"Now, we want to replicate the choice tests you both did a few minutes ago," she says, pulling out two coins and placing them on the small white table. "Sit, please."

The two sit and watch each other before they both reach out to grab the 25 TU coin.

"Oh, sorry. Let me take it. No, I'll take it. You stay there, while I … dang it. What if we just leave it? Yeah, that's what I was thinking."

The woman interrupts and says, "One of you has to take it."

"Well, why don't you tell us which one should get which coin?" they say in unison.

"Because it's not my test," she says smiling.

The Franks look at each other.

"We now have access to tons of TUs, right?" they say, looking at the scientist. She nods.

"So it doesn't really matter—"

"Which I pick...." finishes the other.

"So I'll take this one."

"And I'll take the other."

They both look back at the woman and say, "Happy?"

The interns scribble away furiously.

The scientist then pulls out the same two gum wrappers and puts them where the coins were before. The Franks look at each other and the one with the 25 TU coin nods to the other.

"I got first pick, so now it's your turn."

The other nods and takes a gum. They both ask, "What now?"

The scientist stands up and walks towards a door. "I believe you know Spencer? He's the one who picked you up two weeks ago," she says, opening the door and revealing the skinny boy, this time with large white, fake glasses to match the neat, spotless uniform.

"Two weeks!" the two shout.

"Yes. But don't worry—you'll find everything is in order."

"And what about my house?" they both say.

"It has been taken care of."

"'It has been taken care of'? What's that supposed to mean? I never wanted—"

"It means everything will be fine, and you will not be roommates."

Relieved, they both wipe their hands on their pants, before seeing the other copying the motion and dropping their hands.

"He will take you to the OuterCity and organize your schedule."

"Hold on, our schedule?"

"Yes. In the form you signed there was a clause about your activities after the experiment."

"What if I don't want to go?" they both say defiantly.

"Well, in that case, your balance will be decreased by 25% for each infraction."

"You can't do that! It's mine!"

"That's where you're wrong. This experiment lasts for the rest of your lives, and just like how we gave you TUs, we can also take them away. You agreed to all of this in the forms."

I really should have read that, they both think.

"Ready?" asks Spencer. They both nod.

Chapter 10

AFTER DARK

"WE ARE NOT GOING SHOPPING! At this hour?" Spencer says exasperatedly, voice getting higher and higher with every word.

"But we want to!" the Franks say in unison, enjoying the new-found way to annoy Spencer.

"No. I've been down there for almost a whole day waiting for you two to wake up, and now I want to go home."

"But Spencer ..." they both whine with satisfied smiles.

"No," he says, and starts walking back into the center of the dirty street, now illuminated with hovering lights from the building above. Frank is still amazed by how clean this part of the city is. Maybe they clean it specifically for the fifty people that work down in that ... place. That's likely it. Everywhere else in the Inner and OuterCity is littered with mounds of bags, and usually the closer to the InnerCity, the worse it gets. Suddenly an idea dawns on the two Franks, and they look at each other knowingly.

"Ya know, Spencer, it's pretty late," one says, concealing a smile.

"Don't you think I know that?" Spencer snaps.

"Well, do you know what happens in the Outer-City after dark?" the other Frank asks cryptically.

"What happens?" Spencer asks, trying to look annoyed, but seeming concerned.

"He doesn't know!" the Franks loudly whisper to each other, and both nod.

"You know what, I've decided to listen to your request! You're welcome. We will go up this building and get you both BlueScreens, then you will both buy us a private train car back to the OuterCity. I have made up my mind—let's go."

Spencer turns and reopens the large purple doors. Even his fear of the train is overwhelmed by the fear of what might be hiding in the OuterCity after dark. Ignorance can be useful sometimes, both Franks think.

Chapter 11

BLUESCREEN

"This is the brand-new BlueScreen! It has the most storage of any previous BlueScreen!"

"How much storage does it have?" the Franks ask.

"The most!"

"Okay, great, but how much storage is that?" they say again.

The shopbot looks between the two of them, trying to gauge emotion, a joke or perhaps an insult, flicking through webscores and product descriptions, and yet there is no answer to the question. Although the plastic robot isn't real, the awkwardness increases until one Frank breaks the tension, laughing.

"More than the last one!" The two laugh harder than either of them would under normal circumstances. Others in the small store uncomfortably glance over at the still-lightly laughing Franks, who have started to look around the room to ignore the awkwardness.

The shop is simple and clean; no wonder Spencer chose it. Large blue panels on the wall create a stage for the levitating products all around the store. A few others are talking to shop bots and testing the newest models. Next to the sliding glass door, Spencer taps his foot impatiently.

"We'll take two, thank you," the Franks say in unison. The robot's large eyes blink, and a second later, two sleek boxes appear from behind it. Two small doors open on the side of its body, and the long retractable arms extend and twist as its meaningless smile is trained on the Franks. Placing the boxes on the table between them, the arms retract back into the body and the robot asks, "Do you two need help with accounts?"

"Yes, thank you," the Franks say disconcertedly.

It can tell this is a special case. It is a rarity to see anyone without the devices clamped onto their palms, especially two. But the company is always happy to welcome new customers.

BlueScreens have been around for decades; originally, they were a flat, blue screen, but advancements in visual displays have made the now-holographic devices a necessity. The always-increasing variety of options means it has something for everyone. From meeting people to buying both real and imaginary commodities, everything and everyone is accessible. Whatever you want, whenever you need—the most connected ever! Although few recognize the faces they pass every day, when waiting in line or walking in the InnerCity, many hide behind the floating shapes and calming familiarity until the "real world" is nothing more than an annoyance restricting their immersion into the tangled web of flashing lights. When you can be anyone, why be yourself? When you can do everything, why do anything?

The InnerCity does its best to mimic the intoxicating nature of the BlueScreens, filling itself with similar lights and exciting activities. But nothing will compare to the draw of the BlueScreen, because nothing will be as perfect. When your whole life is online, why leave?

Both new accounts are charged for the devices.

Chapter 12

PICK

THIS IS BETTER THAN LIVING with the other but... it feels wrong. Impressive, but wrong. The two look at each other, before looking back at the two identical houses shrouded in darkness. The droopy roofs are perfect copies. The same red paint clings to the walls. The same stairs lead to the same crooked door. Even the grubby old bush is there. No detail was overlooked. They spent thousands of TUs replicating his same, shitty house.

"Tomorrow, you two will get paper messages. The connection out here is always awful, so the BlueScreens can pretty much only tell you the time. Just don't be late."

They nod and look back to the houses. Neither moves. Spencer looks at the two of them, annoyed.

"Go on. Pick!" Spencer says exasperatedly. "I don't have all night, ya know!"

Neither of them moves.

"Okay, here's what we're going to do. One of you take out the coin you picked and flip it. Heads you on the left, tails, you on the right."

They both pull out their coins. Spencer sighs before grabbing one and flipping it. The coin flies into the air, catching the light from the flickering yellow lamps. It hovers for a moment before plummeting back down and landing in his palm. He flips it on the back of his hand and moves his hand away.

"Heads. You on the left—pick or I will."

"Fine, I'll take the original."

"Good. Oh, here's your coin."

Frank takes it, before tossing the coin back into the darkness. "Don't need it anymore, do I?" He smiles, walking to the house. Frank watches the other return to his house.

"As similar as you could make it, it'll never be the same," Frank says, looking back at Spencer.

"Nothing will ever be the same," Spencer comments.

"Damn Spencer, that's depressing!" Frank replies. Spencer just shrugs boredly. He's probably right. They fall into silence as Frank watches the bright lights flick on inside what should be his house.

"Why'd you do it?" Spencer bursts, breaking the silence. Surprised, Frank turns to look at him. He's so young he can't see the reality that presses on everything in the InnerCity and the OuterCity.

"Why do we do anything?"

"Because we are passionate?"

"No. It's because of money. That's the only real value in this world. I took the risk of volunteering because it was better than starving to death or becoming one of those scroungers. I learned pretty fast that the only person that would help me is me. So that's what I decided to do, help myself. I was fired, again, a few days before your experiment, and in that time, it was hell. I knew I couldn't survive with the money I had, but no one would hire me. I didn't have another option. And I thought, what's worse: whatever they have planned, or living like this? And well, you know what answer I decided on."

"And what if what we did turns out to be worse than your life before?"

"How could it be? I have more TUs than I could spend in my life!"

"What about the reductions?"

"I'm sure I can convince whoever is told to do that to just give us warnings or something. I mean they can't just take that away. That's cruel, I earned it."

"So, how would you feel if that person did take it away?"

"They just can't, they won't—or at least, I won't give them a reason to!" Frank takes the coin from his pocket and examines it, turning the shining metal in his fingers, before casually flipping it into the darkness. Spencer looks at him, confused.

"Don't need it anymore, do I? I'm rich!" Frank laughs before strolling confidently into the "new" house.

Chapter 13

ICY EMBRACE

ACROSS REALITIES, FAR FROM the blue mist, far from Frank, the city changes.

The people burn and boil in the streets of the city, demanding an answer, demanding a solution, but as the hours pass their anger begins to fade. It is replaced by cold, hunger, and fear. They shout until all that's left of their anger are smoldering coals that are soon replaced by the harsh, icy reality that is fear.

Fear blankets the city—crawling out of corners and alleyways until the last flame of anger is smothered in its icy embrace. It grows ever closer in the shadows, and when everything else is gone, it remains

Deep in the cavern, the show continues.

Chapter 14

25% REDUCTION

"GOD DAMMIT!"

Frank's morning "alarm" is normally the dancing lights from the window, but today, the other house blocks the slim rays of the sun. Frank jumps out of his bed and runs to get dressed. He hurriedly unlocks his door and flings it open. A small scrap of paper is stuck to it. Peeling it off, Frank reads it.

"Good morning, Frank. Today is the first day of your new life! Both of you must be at *The Blue Lily*, located in Stonewood Plaza, at 9:30 am, or you will receive a penalty."

It's 11:45 am.

Locking the door as quickly as he can, Frank trips over his laces on the uneven stairs and runs into the dusty street. Faces peer out of doorways and around corners and Frank is buffeted by the wind as he gasps in the dry scratchy air.

He can't lose the money before he even gets the chance to spend it! The long streets seem never-ending as each turn ends in another intersection. Red dust billows as Frank skids around a corner and turns towards the train platform. The silver train beeps and the doors start closing. The platform groans under Frank's heavy footfalls as he squeezes through the doors onto the train. Holding his side, Frank collapses into a seat. The train accelerates and they shoot through the city.

The train is almost empty. So there is a reason why they never run them during the day, he thinks. It's incredibly lucky he was able to make it just in time.

Frank unfolds the small paper and scans for the name. *Stonewood Plaza*. Frank consults the small glowing screen.

First stop: *Orangelake Center*

Second stop: *Pink Ridge*

Third stop: *Stonewood Plaza*

Who comes up with these names? The scent of stale coffee fills the compartment, as a voice explains why this cup truly is the best in the InnerCity. Waving the hologram away Frank slides further back in the chair and closes his eyes. Maybe the long sleep wasn't the worst that could have happened.

〰 〰

The musical ding rings through the compartment and the doors slide open. Frank files out onto the large bustling platform. Lights and enticing smells fill the air as holographs and speakers simultaneously vie for his attention.

From restaurants to shopping malls and clubs, the InnerCity is full of never-ending entertainment and infatuations. The light-studded buildings all sport landing docks and ads for a variety of items. The Zipers fly through the air like a horde of wasps. And the people! Bustling and shuffling past him are hundreds of people, each covered in the brightest colors imaginable—they don't even look real. One group is covered in yellow feathers, bustling along the plaza, looking more like a flock of birds than humans. And on the other side, large flashing spherical hats bob among the fray. Everything gives the idea of a person, but no one's shoulders are that pointy, head that round, or legs so … puffy. And the buttons, why would anyone need so many buttons?

Frank weaves his way through the people to a flashing sign, *The Blue Lily*. Ducking into the store, he is met with a blanketing smell of silky sweet flowers. A small army of pill-shaped powder-blue robots roll to greet him. They turn to him expectantly.

"Hello…."

"Welcome to *The Blue Lily*. How may we assist you?"

"Is there a Frank here?" he asks.

The machines whirl, almost like they're thinking.

"Yes."

Frank waits, but none of them move.

"Uhh, can you take me to him?"

"Yes." The small army springs into action and Frank is swept deeper into the store, shepherded by the robots.

"Frank! There you are!" A pink curtain parts. The other Frank is standing awkwardly on a small pedestal surrounded by robots, scientists, and…

"Spencer? Why are you here?" the newly arrived Frank asks.

"I was assigned to both of you until you get your bearings, remember? I will be with you all the time." He looks at Frank standing awkwardly in the fabric on the pedestal. "Believe me. I'm thrilled," he adds drily.

"And everyone else?" asks Frank

"They're just monitoring," Spencer says, leaning further back into the circular couch.

"Monitoring what?"

"You." Spencer pauses before straightening and saying, "Oh yeah, I just remembered … you're late." Tapping the palm of his hand he turns on his BlueScreen. Spencer's eyes glaze over as the boxes shift following his eyes. A moment later he says, "I've just reduced your account by 25%."

"What! Spencer, it was you! Come on, it wasn't even my fault!" Frank shouts defensively.

"You were late."

"Ya see, I'm trying to tell you that was not my fault!" The other scientists have turned to watch him and are now furiously tapping on small tablets. "In fact, it's your fault!" Frank continues, changing tactics. "You didn't let me have the window side and now no light comes into my room and the stupid streets are different every day and …."

"Hey! Excuses will do nothing, Frank," Spencer says pointedly, shaking his head in mock disappointment.

Who does this pompous asshole think he is? Spencer should have told him last night that he was going to be reducing the accounts! And why on earth are they letting some kid do it? A child, who clearly cannot see reason! But as Frank's inner turmoil grows, Spencer leans back into the strange coach and smugly waits for Frank to say something, hand still hovering threateningly over the BlueScreen.

How could so much be gone so fast, and for such a small mistake? It's not fair, he earned that. He forgets the world around him as his face grows hot and anger starts to build in his body. The white coats lean in closer watching his reaction to this test, gauging his tendencies. They wait for a result. Suddenly a small cough from behind him serves as a reminder of everyone around him, and Frank releases his fist, lowering them to his side.

"Whatever. It doesn't even matter," Frank grouches, slouching into one of the pink chairs defeatedly.

It does matter, but if he says anything, Spencer will surely take more. The tapping intensifies as Frank watches his feet in embarrassment and defeat. The room falls silent except for the endless tapping until an annoyed voice breaks the silence.

"Am I done yet?" The other Frank is still standing on the pink pedestal wearing ghastly polka-dotted pants and a bulky purple jacket stretched tightly over his stomach.

"Mmm, yeah sure, you can get down," Spencer says, distractedly.

"Thanks," Frank says, groaning and carefully stepping off the platform, wobbling slightly in the tall purple shoes.

"How about you give it a try, Frank?" Spencer says, turning back to look at Frank, still watching his own feet.

"Me?" Frank says, looking up after a moment to see everyone watching him.

"Naw, I'll pass," he says, trying to sound non-chalant, but looking back to see the clearly humiliated Frank being led away by the small robots.

"Frank, that wasn't really a request," Spencer says, slowly reaching to open his BlueScreen.

"Fine. I'll do it."

"Good!" Spencer says, while all the others tap more incessantly into the tablet. Two small robots wheel up to Frank and begin to roll into his legs until he stands and begrudgingly follows them out.

Chapter 15

POLKA DOTS

A SMALL METAL DOOR CLOSES Frank into the small claustrophobic room. The high ceiling and thin walls give him the impression of being examined by a microscope. This would have been less uncomfortable if he had not been stripped naked by the small robots. The smell of lavender is overpowering as the wall occasionally spritzes into his face.

The wall starts to hum, and a thin panel slides away revealing neatly stacked clothes in a small compartment. First is a spiky pair of padded black pants with confusing mounds of fabric at his knees, but the shiny black material is stretched tight over the rest of his legs. Frank shifts uncomfortably as his feet have started to swell slightly. Next is a bright green shirt with sleeves that spiral in thick ringlets from his shoulders. It itches. Finally, a second compartment opens, revealing a tall hat and pair of flat shoes. Everything also happens to be covered in rainbow circles, similar to those Spencer had been wearing when they first met, except so much worse. He angrily puts them on and waits in the small room.

This is utterly humiliating. The door unlatches and slowly opens to reveal more robots waiting patiently. Upon seeing him they start rolling into his legs again to force him to move. With every step, the pants squeak and stretch painfully. He slowly makes his way back to the pink room and waits. The thin curtains open, revealing the group all sitting on the soft chairs. The other Frank is even sleeping on one of the fluffy pink chairs. Frank is pushed forward and repeatedly bumped until he steps onto the short pink pedestal. The room is silent except for the tapping on the tablets.

"So what do you think, Frank?" asks one of the robots in a monotone voice.

"What even are these?" Frank asks, pointing at one of the blue circles on his stomach.

"They're polka dots. Aren't they great?" says one of the small robots.

"No."

"Spence says it's all the rage," interjects one of the white coats, who had seemingly taken a break from his endless tapping.

Spencer nods knowingly.

"It's cutting edge!" says another, although this one sounds more sarcastic.

"Yeah, you look great, Frank!" says another with a smirk. That was definitely an insult.

"I want to take it off now please," Frank says through clenched teeth to little robots. The robots turn to the rest of the group, waiting for one of them to make a decision.

"You're getting it," Spencer says, matter-of-factly.

Frank shrugs. At least he can leave now.

"Everything the other Frank got they will send to you as well. This was, honestly, just for fun," Spencer finishes, smiling. The rest of the group looks amused. One even stealthily opens his bluescreen and captures an image of Frank standing slouched in the ridiculous outfit. Carefully stepping off the platform, Frank takes one last look at himself in the wide mirror. Or what was himself.

Polka dots? Really? Frank hurries out of the room, following the small robots.

Chapter 16

WORDS ALONE

ACROSS REALITIES, FAR FROM the blue mist, far from Frank, the city changes.

Nothing is the same. Nothing will ever be how it was before. But maybe, the right person could bring it back. They could bring everything back. The lights, the music, the never-ending enjoyment, and the burden-free life.

But that's not all the city was, not for everyone. For every new item, there was time and labor spent. For every light, there was a hidden cost; they were just too blind to see it.

The district leaders of the city have started to gather. They have begun to form a group. To find someone that can finally fill the dead air. They present themselves as best as possible, donning tall hats and flamboyant outfits before taking to the stage.

But no one turns to listen. No one looks at them as they begin to speak. Without TUs, they have lost their power. The tantalizing TUs that they once dangled over the city's head are now useless. Their words are nothing more than that—words—and no one could ever control the city with words alone.

Deep in the cavern, the show continues.

Chapter 17

SURPRISING? NO.

THE TWO WALK INTO A LARGE warehouse laden with large shopping bags led by Spencer.

"What are you two interested in today?" asks a woman whose name tag introduces her as "Jes." The break from shop bots is refreshing, as most stores are overrun by the small wheely annoyances. Instead, they are assisted by a middle-aged woman with short light purple hair who, while impeccably dressed, gives the impression of one seeking to create an illusion. Of course, that could be said of much of the InnerCity.

"We're both getting apartments soon and we need furnishings," one Frank explains.

"What type of look are you both going for?"

"I want," they both start, before looking at each other.

"Sorry, go ahead," Frank sighs, nodding to the other Frank.

"Thanks. I want something soft and colorful, or just the newest thing you have," he says, absent-mindedly looking around the store at the hovering merchandise.

"Alrighty," says the woman, typing into a flat disk.

"That'll be right this way. I will have my associate take you there."

Another woman appears almost out of thin air and looks at the two men, both dressed in dirty brown pants and somewhat white shirts but carrying bags from the most expensive and sought-after stores in the city. Maybe they're making a fashion statement. The two simultaneously shift uncomfortably. Jes clears her throat. With a jolt, the new attendant motions for the other Frank to follow her.

"And for you?" Jes asks, turning to Frank.

He pauses, then, "I want something unique, and different."

"Uhh, okay," she says typing into the pad. Frank awkwardly looks around the store to fill the silence. Chairs and tables of all sizes hover throughout the store, gently spinning in place. The sets range from silky red couches to scaly lime green chairs. The store itself seems confused about what to do. Every light in the store is aimed at the hovering furniture so that the ground itself is only lit by strips of luminescent tape. And once again, in the corner, stands Spencer tapping his foot.

"Here we go, I think I've got something," she says, holding up the pad. "Would this be what you're interested in? It's one of a kind, handmade. It is considerably more expensive, however."

The collection she's talking about is, in fact, unique. Everything is shaped to look like a cloud and is made from a silky iridescent fabric.

"Can I see it?" asks Frank.

"Yes, right this way," she says excitedly.

From the way she quickly moves through the aisles, he can tell this might be the first time someone has been interested enough to venture this far into the store. When they finally arrive, she looks nervously between his face and the furniture. Now unsure of her decision she quickly adds, "If you don't like it, we have many other options …."

"No, I'll take it."

"Great! Not many appreciate quality pieces like these; most tend not to understand that these are not intended to be replaced every few weeks. When you came into the store, I couldn't help noticing—is he your twin?"

"No, we are actually …," he thinks, trying to find the right phrasing. "We're actually the same person."

"Oh … okay." She doesn't totally understand. Thinking for a moment, a realization takes hold, and she adds, "That's why you two kept interrupting the other, and why you wanted something unique."

How does she know? "You're not from the Inner-City, are you?"

She shifts uncomfortably and pulls the tablet up.

"I didn't mean to—"

"Sign here and they will be delivered soon," she says, readopting a controlled smile and pleasant indifference. He can't say no to her now, after what he said. Sighing, Frank signs the screen, and he can almost feel the TUs being ripped from him.

Surprising? No. Disappointing? Yes.

Chapter 18

FEAR NOT

Across realities, far from the blue mist, far from Frank, the city changes.

The city does nothing but wait. No direction, no purpose. But sitting and waiting for things to happen makes everything so much slower. And the city is doing nothing but waiting. Waiting for a leader. Waiting for an answer. Waiting for someone, anyone, to tell them what to do and when to do it. But no one is coming. The governor isn't going to do anything, and the divisional leaders can't. So they all do nothing but sit and wait. They wait until one voice speaks up. The ones who had taken Frank and made him disappear someplace in the city.

"Fear not!" Well, that's too late, he thinks. "We will have an answer soon."

"How soon?" one yells back at the small, crudely constructed stage with the small podium and a thin, greasy-looking teenager with blue latex gloves.

"Someone will inform you when an answer is found."

"You didn't answer the question!" a woman shouts from deep in the crowd. They look exhausted. Flimsy red tents have sprung up sporadically in the streets; this is the first time they've all emerged. They're all here to listen to him.

"Look, I'll be honest with you all," the young man says, lowering his grating voice and looking down, seemingly in sorrow, "I don't know when we will have the answer, I don't know how long it will take, and I can't tell you how we're doing it. But I can say, I … we are just as frightened as the rest of you. You must trust that science will find the answer faster than beating it out of him. Even though some of you would really like that." A slight chuckle rises from the audience, but the boy continues, "I trust in all of you to give us the time we need to find the truth. Justice will be served! I am Spencer Conamis, and I promise to get you the answer you want, and the justice we deserve!"

The crowd spontaneously erupts into loud applause, and it takes a moment before Spencer realizes they are cheering for him! He folds the small piece of paper with the carefully created speech and tucks it quickly into his pocket.

Deep in the cavern, the show continues.

Chapter 19

A LOSING BATTLE

"This is a one-bedroom, 850 square feet apartment; it has two bathrooms, an entertainment room, and a balcony overlooking the city."

"How much?" Frank asks. Ever since Spencer reduced his account, he grows more and more worried about every purchase, until he becomes paralyzed with indecision.

"It is within your price range," Spencer interjects knowingly.

"Is there a second apartment?" asks the other Frank.

"Yes, the other also has a larger entertainment room, although it does not have a balcony," the sales agent says, smiling widely.

"Great, they'll take it!" Spencer says. "You two get comfortable while I pay." Frank watches nervously as the two step outside—it better not be too much.

They both stand still as the circular door closes like two large petals. As soon as the door is closed, they both pull off the ridiculously large jackets Spencer had forced them to wear and drop them unceremoniously onto the floor. The two small hats, however, are firmly clipped to their heads. After a bit of pulling, the two give up and begin to look through the lavish apartment.

It comes fully equipped with color-changing walls, programmable windows, and a kitchen. One of the Franks ambles to the silver wall dial and spins it absentmindedly. The walls flash, spanning every possible color, before finally landing on a deep ruby red. The hue looks familiar, and like a spark, it ignites a memory deep in their minds.

A drop of blood falls to the dusty ground. It rises in thick plumes as Frank shuffles to avoid another punch. His heart beats fast and hard in his ribcage, and he has already begun to sweat. This isn't fair. Why can't they just leave him be? Another swing. This one lands. Frank stumbles back, clenching his chin as more of the hot red blood drops to the ground. Piercing laughter rises and Frank's face grows hot. His fists burn. If they would just leave him alone... Frank swings, his fist collides, causing the other to stumble back; Frank hits again, and again, and again. The shouting grows louder, but they have turned to cheers, cheers for him. He hits again, harder, faster. His body burns as the adrenaline courses through him. He is still hitting.

They cheer louder as more blood drops to the dusty ground. Frank doesn't stop, he can't. His fist grows hot as he holds back a smile. The other falls to the ground in a crumpled heap, but he keeps hitting.

The cheering stops but he doesn't, he can't. They tell him to stop, plead with him. But he can't. He doesn't stop until he is pulled away by a teacher. Frank is tossed out of a door onto the searing asphalt. Hot, dry air floods his nose and the chalky sensation of dust slides across his palms as he rubs them together. In the dark shadow of a tall, spine-like tower, Frank sits crumpled on the cracked road and looks up to hundreds of windows, faces peering out to look at him not with concern but amusement.

The wall flickers and the memory fades as they look uncomfortably around the room. Another dial is stuck to the opposite wall, but neither moves to touch it. Frank looks down to see his fist clenched into a tight ball; he shakes it loose. Trying to not meet the other's eyes, Frank looks up. Instead of a ceiling, there is more space. The star-shaped bed is visible through the clear ceiling. A large chandelier dangles above the bed and casts a star-shaped shadow into the living room.

In the corner, a clear escalator silently revolves.

The two walk around the square room, amazed by the exorbitant and unnecessary additions to the spacious apartment. The smart system in the dining room table makes the kitchen useless. With a push of a button, food is ordered from one of the hundreds of nearby restaurants. Frank groans: this too will cost money. The entertainment room is covered with lights that, when turned on, create immersive holographic images. These are so entrancing that the Franks watch them in awe for ten minutes, before snapping out of their trance and quickly turning off the device.

Anything they could possibly need, all on this first floor. He could spend his whole life here, never once wanting or needing to leave. After examining the living area, both bathrooms, and the kitchen, the Franks split; the other goes to test the mattress in the bedroom, while Frank looks out onto the balcony. Two thin glass panels are the only divider between him and the 132-floor drop to the street below.

The city only really comes alive at night. The darkness is a perfect canvas for the dazzling lights. Frank touches a smooth dial with his hand, and the panels glide open. The decorative fruit bowl flies off the kitchen table, as a frigid gust of wind rushes through the opening. The hat leaps from Frank's head and disappears into the deep abyss between the buildings. Eyes watering from the air, he steps out onto the balcony and watches the city.

Music resonates from deep within the city. From the high vantage point, the flashing lights from the center bounce off the shiny buildings and look brighter than the sun. The faint sound is promptly drowned out by the wind as it returns with a vengeance, upset to have been forgotten. The hollow, echoing sigh fights with the music for superiority. As the two sounds compete, they create something new, a ghostly imitation of each other. As the wind carries the music further from its source, it transforms the sound into its own sorrowful mourning, not wanting to be forgotten as it once again fades into nothing.

Deep in the heart of the city the music pounds on, unfazed by the gust of wind that had momentarily changed it. Who else had heard the wind's attempt to overthrow the music? Who else had seen the hopeless war the wind wages, forever fighting a losing battle? Who else listened?

Chapter 20

PARALYZED

Across realities, far from the blue mist, far from Frank, the city changes.

As the last rays of light fade, what's left of the city becomes quiet. The remaining generators have gone silent. No music, no lights, nothing to fill the gaping darkness. So, in that void, a different sound returns. The wind howls in the empty air where the city once stood. The howling grows louder and louder as the city grows quieter. With nothing in its way, no obstacles in its path, it grows stronger. Below, the people are listening; they hear the wind asking them where they've gone, but no one can answer, because no one knows.

They don't know why it is gone. They don't know who has taken it. They don't know what to do. The fear of decision paralyzes the city. As the wind howls louder, it brings the red dust billowing behind it. Everything and everyone are covered in a thick brown glaze.

Deep in the cavern, the show continues.

Chapter 21

YOU SHOULD HAVE SEEN YOUR FACE

A LOUD RING RESOUNDS IN the apartment, and Frank ignores it again. Another, more persistent ring, and then a third, fourth, and fifth ringing in fast succession. He rolls over and sandwiches his head in between a fluffy pillow, but the ringing switches to a loud pounding, followed by an annoying squeaking voice shouting his name. Frank sighs and sits up on the soft stair bed.

"I'm coming! Relax!" Frank shouts, rubbing his face tiredly. He stands on the warm glass floor and the wall begins to glow a soft yellow as he blinks lazily. Frank stretches before walking a few feet to the escalator to descend. He stretches again before stepping off and walking to the large petal doors, pressing the small dial to open them just an inch.

"Good morning, Frank," says Spencer sourly. "Or should I say good afternoon?"

"Hey, I know for a fact that I didn't have anything for today," Frank says, smugly putting his eye to the small hole.

"Yeah, well things change. Get ready now and hurry up."

"Uhh. Do I have to?" Frank grumbles

"You could always skip," Spencer says with mock innocence, but he slowly raises his left hand towards his BlueScreen and inches towards the]button.

"No, no," Frank says, panicked. "I'll be ready in a minute, just hold on."

Spencer smiles smugly as the doors close and Frank can hear his foot lightly tapping as he scrambles up the revolving stairs to the dresser.

Everything is so ugly. He rifles through the drawer before finally grabbing the same thing he wore the day before and hastily putting it on. Sliding back down the stairs, he slicks his thinning hair back onto his head. A moment later the petals open wider and reveal Frank breathing heavily. Spencer smiles.

"Finally, you took so long! Let's go get the other Frank."

"Can I wait here?"

Spencer pretends to consider it for a moment before saying, "No" with a smile. Frank drags his feet as he follows Spencer down the small hall, looking longingly at the doors sliding shut.

Spencer reaches the other petal-like door and presses the small purple button next to the wall. From within he can hear it ringing loudly, the same sound that had woken him. Spencer rolls his eyes and leans against the wall as he keeps pressing the button. Frank shrugs and leans onto the wall, knowing that the other Frank will take just as long as he did. Finally, the other Frank shouts, "I'm coming, relax!" This is followed by the sound of someone falling out of bed, then painfully walking to the door, opening it an inch, and peering through, just like he did.

"Good morning, Frank," says Spencer sourly. "Or should I say good afternoon?"

"Hey, I know for a fact that I didn't have anything for today," Frank says smugly, putting his eye to the small hole. He sees Frank standing against the wall.

"Frank?" the other asks.

"Yeah, we have to go do something. He didn't tell me what, but go get ready."

"But we—"

"I know we weren't supposed to have anything today, but now we do apparently."

"Uhh, fine. I'll be there in a bit."

"Hurry," Spencer yells, as the door closes again.

Frank closes his eyes, thinking of the bed back in his apartment. It is calling his name. Would it be that bad if he blew Spencer off and went back to sleep? His answer comes in the form of Spencer standing an inch from his face and yelling "Wake up!" as loud as he could muster. Frank shouts and jumps, hitting his head on the low ceiling.

"Why, Spencer!" he says, rubbing the back of his head in indignation. But Spencer is gasping for breath between his uproarious laughter.

"You," Spencer starts laughing, harder again, before regaining composure enough to say, "You should have seen your face!" The petal door opens and the other Frank stands looking in confusion at Spencer clutching his stomach and at Frank, still rubbing his head.

"Uhh, I'm ready."

"Come on then, you two," Spencer says. Still chuckling at his own joke, he starts to quickly walk down the hall to the large elevator. Now accustomed to his speed, the two Franks follow close behind, until Spencer suddenly stops to push the button.

"So can you tell us where we're going?"

"No."

"Will you tell us what we're going to be doing?" the other Frank asks

"No."

"Can you tell us why we're going there?"

"No! No, no, no. Now be quiet!" Spencer snaps, crossing his arms and tapping his foot impatiently. The two Franks look at each other and roll their eyes as the small elevator chimes.

Chapter 22

OTHERWORLD

HOW DEEP DOES THIS THING GO? The tunnels beneath *Next: Medical Procedures and Cosmetic Alterations* extend much further than the main hall and even further than the strange experiment rooms. Here, it is so far down that air feels like water in his lungs, and the walls carry a dank fungus smell.

The procession shuffles quietly through the halls. Frank begins to wonder if they are about to see lava or even the other side of the world. Finally, they enter a small dimly lit room with two glistening … eggs? The hollowed-away rocks look like a bite into an apple. The jutted edges and uneven surfaces only differentiate itself from a cave by the stalactites dangling in the corner.

All this rock is in surprising opposition to the pods positioned symmetrically in the room. Their shiny metallic surface is brand new; not even a speck of dust mares its obscenely perfect exterior.

From the little they were told on the long, long trip down they would be entering the "Otherworld" through these state-of-the-art pods. These are obviously the pods.

In the "Otherworld," they will be tested to discover the strength of the human mind. They vaguely alluded to three tests in total, but no one was very forthcoming with more information.

From what they said, the first test will be more primitive. Something would tempt the most animalistic parts of the mind. This thing, although they won't say what it is, may make him lose control over his rational mind.

The other two were similar tests; one would test morality, and the other would test physicality. How exactly they plan on doing this is beyond him. Something else in the contract that they should have read, they both think. They didn't bother to explain what the Otherworld was, but it seems possible he wouldn't have heard of it before. New forms of entertainment always have the InnerCity on its toes. Products advance so fast in the InnerCity that in days they won't be cutting edge anymore.

Regardless of how old the technology is, these couldn't have been here for long. They appear to still be powering up, suggesting that whoever placed the pods here couldn't have left in time. So, where did all the people go? No other tunnels lead to this room, and no one met them in the tunnel. Maybe in the walls. It does look too much like an apple bite. It looks artificial. Only two of the corners have stalactites. They should be in all corners. There must be a divider in the room, with people hiding behind it. Watching. Will he never again be truly alone?

Frank is roughly pushed aside as the others enter the room. The procession of white lab coats files into the room and silently splits into two groups, each attending to one of the eggs. The two Franks look at each other impatiently. Seconds later, a sound of pressurized gas escaping fills the chamber, and the eggs open, revealing a tangle of wires and switches. Of course, it only looks good from the outside. The top shell of the egg has a small window of clear glass, presumably so the lurkers can study them while they are in the "Otherworld."

The two dutifully walk to the pods and are fitted with bulky helmets and wires. Syringes and electrodes are stuck to their arms, and they are slowly lowered into the eggs. Lastly, the lid begins to close and gas hisses into the pod.

As the colors and the world fade, everything else is amplified. The soft gas fills the waning world. It tastes like … pink. Pink, the color of the sun—no, that's yellow. Pink like a clear sky. No, that's blue. Pink like the trees, pink like ice, pink like water, like an apple, like dirt, like clouds, like a lemon… those aren't pink. But it doesn't matter what color it is; the world has faded, and a new light is approaching, like falling down a long dark tunnel, or flying. Maybe both?

Chapter 23

ORB

LANDING IN A GRAY, FOGGY FOREST, the color rushes back. Red and orange leaves cover the ground. Thin white branches reach into the gray thunderous clouds. The air is clean and damp. It smells like decaying leaves and growing underbrush. Like electricity, it feels alive, eternally buzzing.

Pressing his hand deep into the damp soil, the buzzing surges through his nerves and makes bones vibrate. Recoiling from the buzzing it gets louder. The trees are alive. The ground is alive, the clouds and the rain all breathe as one connected being. For a moment, he was a part of it. Another extremity of the forest. Standing in the small clearing, a figure approaches from the mist. It's him. The two stare at each other.

"Come on, this way." Nodding and stepping into the mist behind Frank, the two fall in stride.

The silence of the forest is eerie. In the city, nothing ever stops, no one rests. Even in the OuterCity, something's always happening. But here, here it feels as if nothing has happened in eons. It seems as if they are disturbing some long slumber. They are intruders, waking the peaceful forest to blunder through its mist and trample the undergrowth.

Another small clearing comes into view. Here, as well, the leaves are strewn about. This must have been where the other Frank had woken. But in this clearing, there is a table. A small table. The dark wood has delicately carved leaves along the edge and the legs look like frozen air, twisting and silky. On top of the table is a small, speckled bowl, the same color as the dark sky above. Inside is a thin sheet of … paper. Picking up the delicate sheet he reads the first line.

1. *Find the other Frank.*

So that is why Frank came to find him.

2. *Welcome, this is a scavenger hunt. You will both be searching for three yellow orbs; these are the points. You will want to keep the orbs more than anything but return them to the bowl to win. All three must be returned at the same time to win the game.*

3. *Good luck*

"That's it?"

"Yep."

"So, can we work together?" Frank asks to the air. They both wait for a response, but the only change is a slight breeze. Frank looks back at the small paper.

4. No collaborating. It is a contest.

"Alright then. See ya, Frank," he says, as the other turns and disappears into the mist.

"Yep, good luck."

Huh, where to look first? Frank bends to look under the table. Chuckling to himself, Frank sees a small palm-sized orb stuck to the bottom of the table. The orb emanates a soft yellow glow and hums gently. He reaches one hand towards the orb, but as soon as his finger touches its surface, everything stops. The world is frozen; only the continuous gentle humming of the orb remains. Frank detaches it. The small thing feels warm, it feels alive. The electric buzz courses through it. The same electric humming that the rest of the forest is a part of.

Snapping out of his trance, Frank looks up—this is how to find them. Shoving the orb into his pocket, Frank kneels to the ground, pressing his hands into the damp earth. The electric buzz courses through him, but instead of recoiling, he waits. And the electricity accepts him. Image after image flashes before his eyes, a cluster of red mushrooms, one gnarly tree, a small ratty bush at the roots of a sapling, through another thicket of trees, a left at a pile of leaves, and into the barren branches of a young tree, the yellow glow just visible through its twiggy arms before it's gone again.

Scouring the clearing with his eyes, they land on a cluster of red beneath a tree. Running towards them, he looks down. The small knobs are red with pinpricks of white and are clustered tightly against the trunk. Yes, it's the same. He squints through the trees. Yes, there right there is the old gnarly tree! Leaving the mushrooms he rushes to the tree. The thick white bark feels like paper and from under its branches, the tree seems to be pulling itself towards something. A cold breeze rushes past and Frank grips the trunk. There! Just visible through the fog is the small ratty bush. Running towards it, Frank sees the thicket of trees, left at the leaves and finally, there it is. Barely visible through the twiggy branches is one yellow, humming orb.

Gently plucking the orb from the tree it hums happily, as if saying hello. Shoving this one deep into his pockets before freezing again, he surveys the surroundings.

Chapter 24

PULL

How had he gotten here? Nothing but the shimmering yellow surface occupies his thoughts as he ambles deeper into the trees. Without a care in the world, he admires leaves and sticks. Nothing will ever ruin this.

In both his pockets lay the orbs. His hands are still warm from the touch. Following the trees, he walks. And walks. And walks. Until finally, he reemerges into the clearing with the table. He doesn't notice until the side of his leg hits the sharp corner. Crying out in surprise, he snaps out of his trance—just in time too. Frank leaps from behind him. Slamming into the ground, Frank stutters, "What are you—" Thrashing wildly, he breaks free. Feeling his pockets desperately, an orb is missing.

He breathes heavily as the loss overcomes him. Desperately searching the ground for the precious orb, he panics before looking up. A little distance away, Frank stands looking intently at the orb in his hand. Shouting and running at him, Frank knocks the other to the ground. Grabbing the orb, he pulls with all his strength. It doesn't budge. Frank's dirty fingernails cling to the orb, pulling it closer—he must have dug to find the last orb.

Letting go of the orb, Frank pauses before punching the other square in the jaw. He burns with anger as he hits harder, breathing heavier. Then another and another and another, until Frank returns the blows, his hand still clenched around the orb. The metal surface feels so cold as it hits his throat. So cold as it hits his nose with a defining crack. So very cold as it hits him in the temple.

The cold metal is all around him; the pod contracts and Frank can't breathe. The helmet falls off and is wrapped around his neck. Opening the small door, he stumbles out of the pod, catching his breath before screaming. Screaming so loud it fills the rocky room and fills his thoughts; nothing but betrayal crosses his mind.

As his lungs fail and the scream quiets to a rasp, his mind fades to nothing; it is replaced by another thought. Revenge. There, sleeping peacefully, is Frank in his egg. Without a thought, he rips open the lid. The pink gas spills out but the helmet is still on his head. Wrapping a black cord around his neck, Frank pulls. The small holo-cores that illuminate the room hum as the small version of Frank stumbles. He drops the orb and starts clawing at his neck attempting to fight off the phantom assailant, worlds away. He pulls harder, tightening the cord. Frank's face begins to turn purple and the small image falls to the ground. Life slowly leaves him as his image flickers and fades in the game.

In the corner of the room, a commotion erupts just out of sight, but the only sound Frank can hear is the humming of the orbs. So close now. Another good pull should do it.

Something is wrong; the image is becoming more saturated, still crumpled to the ground but growing brighter. Hands push Frank away from the pod and force him back into the other pod. No, he was so close! All that work can't end now. The helmet is forced back on his head and the strap is pulled tight. More hands push him into the pod and close the door. With all people gone, Frank punches the hard glass. But as the first cracks appear, the pink, sick, sweet gas fills the pod, and Frank falls back into the Otherworld.

Frank's crumpled figure lays before him as the mist retreats. All three orbs lay scattered on the ground. As he collects the orbs, all the anger and fear dissipate as he holds the warm humming creatures close.

He did it, he won. All that's left is to turn them in. Turn them in. The rules had clearly stated he must turn in all the orbs—but why would he do that? He wants to keep them. He earned it. He deserves it. The distance to the table stretches. What seconds ago was a few feet now looks impossible. Why should he turn them in? To win this stupid game? Finish their experiment?

The electric pull from deep within the forest reaches out. It twists into long invisible cords that slither up his legs. From the table another pull reaches out, hoping to move him closer. The icy humming snakes engulf his body. They pull, hard. As each grows stronger, he hangs in the balance, suspended between the two choices.

With nothing left for the strings to pull, they begin to pull him apart. Will the sheer inability to decide kill him? Maybe one will break, and he will be flung to the right answer, but as he waits for the decision to be made for him, they do not break. They do not splinter or unwind. They just … keep … pulling.

Caught in the balance of two unwavering wills, both from within himself. Then another snake, pulling down. Pulling itself closer. Eyes glimmering with hate and face set with resolve, he pulls himself closer. Frozen, Frank watches the pale, greedy thing grow closer.

The cords break. Frank is flung. Flying, sprinting, both cords falling to the ground. Frank is running, running, running to the table. Running away from the forest, away from howling creatures crumpled on the forest floor. Away from the mist and towards victory. Watching the three beautiful orbs roll into the bowl and fade away. As the forest is flooded with the sweet mist that leaks from the crack in the glass. The humming of the orbs changes into the mechanical grinding of the lid opening and the warm glow of the lights swinging loosely above the pod. Sitting up, Frank sees himself again, a perfect reflection. He freezes in apprehension.

Two mirrors had been placed in front of both pods. A thin curtain separating the two flutters, almost imperceptibly. For now, the mirrors are enough to fool them. Like the uncertainty when they first met, neither can tell each other apart. A perfect reflection, or himself?

It is impossible to tell. The fragile curtain thickens and strengthens, although they are both awake, neither can see that no matter what they become, they can never escape the reality of their situation. Although they are no longer the same, they still only see a copy of themselves.

Chapter 25

FALLING

"SORRY," FRANK SAYS, clearing his throat.

"Yeah."

They sit in silence, huddled against the cave wall. The numbing cold of the wall seeps into the air, chilling their bones and forcing them to wrap thin blankets tighter around themselves. A flurry of people blur the cave into one continuous stream of motion as the minutes tick past. Someone moves closer, and the two are corralled back to the pods and laid down inside the chambers. Wires and electrodes are again attached and switches flipped. The lid closes. Finally, silence.

The people outside the pod become distant as the gas reappears. The nothingness returns, and the blissful fall into the darkness returns. If only he could stay here forever; but, like before, the mist appears in place of the darkness. The peace is swept away by a strong icy wind as the world materializes.

The two stand, frozen like ice, atop a tall mossy stone bridge. Any other time, or to anyone else, it might be pretty—beautiful even. But it all seems wrong. The two lean over the edge and look down into the gray fog below. As if perfectly on cue, the thin wisps of fog disappear revealing a set of perfectly straight train tracks running under the bridge and into the distance. These aren't like anything in the InnerCity or OuterCity—other than the two Franks, there is nothing but silent empty space pressing in around them. Words materialize from the mist and hover just over the gap:

Welcome to the second game. In a moment, a train will appear. It will not stop or slow down. To win, you must save the people below. Good luck.

The blare of the horn blasts in the distance and makes the two jump. Spinning to see the light growing sharper from the mist, the horn erupts again, this time closer.

Voices screech through the fog pleading with the Franks to help them. Confused, Frank scans the opaque surroundings. He can't see them. Frank continues scouring the mist, waiting for something to appear. The other looks over the edge of the bridge in horror.

The people, five in total are stuck on the tracks, screaming for someone to save them. Finally realizing what's happening, Frank too grasps the edge of the bridge and looks down in equal horror. The train is going so fast; why doesn't it slow down? Frank looks back into the mist, desperately searching for something, anything, to stop the train. Another blast of the horn, this time just mere meters from the bridge—a shuffle, a yell, a slip, then falling.

Chapter 26

SAND

GRINDING BONES IS NOT DISSIMILAR to the feeling of sand in teeth. The hard, gritty substance cracking, then splintering into dust. But sand does not scream. Sand does not cry out for help. Sand does not feel the agony of the grinding wheels slowly inching forward, chewing it into powder. Sand cannot stop a train.

Frank can.

Through a gap between the wheels, Frank watches as the other climbs down from the bridge and humbly receives praise from the five people he rescued. Frank had seen the one solution he would not have dared to act on. Frank had pushed him off the bridge. It was generated so this exact act would stop the train. But why?

Pinned under the train car, watching through the cracks, Frank waits for freedom. But death will not come. All of this is just a simulation, but the weight of the train above feels so real. The hot, dripping oil slides down his face. He bites his cheek, and the metallic taste of blood fills his mouth. His head spins as the train presses the air out of his lungs. It will end soon. But how fast is soon? Not fast enough. How long will they make him wait, trapped under a mountain of steel, bones ground to pulp, skin burning from the scalding pipes with electric wires prickling his skin? Will this ever end? Was this all there has ever been? Burning and grinding, digging, and stretching. Everything is just pain. What could be taking so long?

Finally, the mist returns, the train disappears, and the pod reforms.

Chapter 27

CONGRATULATIONS

Frank sits, frozen. Hands reach in from the outside, but it's no use. He doesn't move. He can't. His bones are ground to mush, muscles torn and skin burned by the searing pipes. Regardless, they pull him from the pod and lean him against the wall, his mind reeling. More shuffling and noises fill the room. But Frank isn't listening. The blaring of the horn resonates in his head like the beat of a drum. Pounding and insistent. On and on.

"Our apologies—one of the pods has been damaged too much for the third game," says one of the white coats who appeared from the fake stone wall.

"What does that mean?" says the other Frank.

A slick-looking man in a pristine coat excitedly speaks up: "We could have them do the physical test in the real world, to complete the experiment!"

"No," Frank interrupts, still slumped against the wall. The muttering mass falls silent.

"Frank. You have to, that was the whole point of the split. We need accurate data."

"You can take your data and shove it right up your—"

"Frank! Just do what they say," says a familiar voice from across the room. He looks up to see the other Frank look at his shoes sheepishly.

"What?" Frank says, and for the first time, he sees the other Frank as something else. Not someone on the same side as him or someone who will always be there, even if it gets annoying, but now as someone who is a pawn, who only does what he is told. If he would just look up, for once if he would just look up and see the world around him. Look up, Frank, he wills. But no. The other Frank won't.

"I don't care about your rules anymore."

"But Frank…" Spencer says, menacingly moving his hand closer to his BlueScreen.

"Take it. I've worried about money more than I have in the past thirty years! I survived before; I'll survive again. This, whatever it is, isn't living," Frank finishes, and resolutely crosses his arms in indignation, hoping that it might help his resolve.

But as Spencer opens his BlueScreen and slowly begins reducing his account, it is all Frank can do not to cry out for him to stop. The number continues to decrease until Spencer finally realizes that this really isn't going to work. He stops to look at Frank, more confused than ever. Silence fills the small cavern as eyes shift, unsure of what to do.

"Well, then," one says, clearing her throat with an awkward cough, "Congratulations Frank!" Polite applause resounds in the cavern. "In that case, I will notify the others and you can both proceed to the party."

"What party?" Frank asks, looking up from his shoes for the first time.

"The party for your victory of course! You're famous! Huge BlueScreen viewership! And just 30 seconds—perfect! Nobody got bored and turned us off! We—you—are trending everywhere! Follow us. You too," she says sourly to the Frank who is still leaning against the wall.

Like white ants, the group files into a line and prepares to enter the tunnel. Someone nudges Frank and he begrudgingly steps into line and follows the others up the long tunnel. His body remembers that it still works, sort of.

Chapter 28

IMMORTALIZED

Music and shouting voices grow progressively louder as they continue up the slow incline. As they near the end of the tunnel the sound becomes deafening, and they stumble into the same large room as before. But now, instead of screens and tangled wires, lights and people spin in a dizzying imitation of joy.

Fabrics whoosh and spin in an ever-changing dance. They dance, they laugh, and they spin. They spin so much they fall into each other, laughing as they get up, and start spinning again. The world fades away and all that is left is the spinning and laughing.

Someone stumbles out of the fray and catches sight of the two Franks standing awkwardly in the tunnel's mouth. The man calls something out and in a singular motion the spinning stops as they stare at the new arrivals. Someone cuts the music, and for a moment, there is utter silence before the other Frank raises his hand. As if a herd of animals had been released, a wall of sound suddenly slams into the two. Hands reach out and grab them, pulling them deeper into the room. The sound builds, growing into a roar.

"Frank, pleased to meet you. I'm J.C Morgan." A ham-like hand grasps his shoulder and shakes it amicably. Frank stares blankly into the large smiling face. As the silence drags on, his smile falters. The voices are so loud. The man looks uncomfortable. He clears his throat before continuing, "I'm the Governor. But don't worry at all, I'm not here on official business." He winks. The Governor never does any business, official or otherwise, Frank thinks.

Another group descends, all shouting introductions and reaching to shake his hand. On the other side of the room, Frank is lifted onto the crowd's shoulders as they chant his name. Everyone here had been watching. Well, good thing they got the show they wanted. That is all this is, all it ever truly was—just one more way to squeeze entertainment out of every possible crevice. All this was only a matter of time.

Why have we evolved to only see humor in others' suffering? Others' embarrassment? Others' betrayal? Frank turns to the tunnel headed to the surface. There is always a hidden audience to entertain. Whether behind a curtain or through cameras, someone is always watching. The Franks' treachery will never be forgotten. It will be immortalized in the BlueScreen's flickering light until suffering is no longer entertaining.

In other words, it will be immortalized forever.

Chapter 29

CANYON

WITH TIME, ALL WOUNDS HEAL. That's what everyone says. But when the entire world is reenacting your suffering, it never ends. Like reopening a cut as it's about to heal, the pain never really goes away. It only dulls until it is a constant ache. But even the smallest drip of water can create a canyon.

Chapter 30

FOREVER TRAPPED

THE TWO SMALL HOUSES NOW lay forgotten, as no one in that world is left to care about them. The glass bottles are shattered on the stained brown floor. They have lost their shine, and spiders have overtaken the rest of the house. They sit undisturbed, waiting in their carefully woven traps for prey. When an unsuspecting bug gets trapped, its fat and shiny body wriggles in the net hopelessly. They spring from their stillness and drape it in soft, sleepy silk until the bug no longer cares that it is trapped. Why would anyone want to leave this place? This drowsiness pervades the space, filling its cracks and corners with the same weary apathy. Forever trapped, but not wanting to leave; never wanting to return to reality.

Chapter 31

ROOTS

THE PURPLE DOORS OF *Next: Medical Procedures and Cosmetic Alterations* swing open as Frank quickly walks into the streets, ignoring the receptionist yelling for him to stop. He walks faster and faster away from *Next,* away from Spencer, and away from Frank. He can't use the train or a Ziper, so the only option is to walk back to his apartment.

There is a reason no one uses the streets anymore. The small part outside of *Next* has indeed been cleaned for the scientists and … the audience. Every other street is nearly impassable. Garbage and discarded merchandise cover the thin road transforming it into an obstacle course. The piles of things sit scattered, making deep trenches and small mountains in the thin space between the shining buildings. It reeks of burnt rubber and rotting food, but here, unlike the OuterCity, it's not coated in the red dust. Instead, it is a wet slippery mess that slides with every step.

Frank stumbles through the streets, occasionally looking up to get a glimpse of the sky above but, as if waiting for the right moment, Zipers soar past, dusting the road with fresh trash that they carelessly toss from their platforms.

Nothing feels real. Everything is synthetic. In the OuterCity, everything is dirty, dull, and dangerous in comparison to the InnerCity. But here, the danger is hidden, traps set for an unsuspecting person to fall into, information and ideas that have been twisted so much they don't resemble the truth anymore. It's too much.

The closer he gets to the apartment building, the stronger the acrid stench grows. Thankfully, it's enough to keep everyone away from these forgotten roads. Being alone is enough to make the smell worth it. Why had he allowed himself to become enthralled by the InnerCity? Frank walks and walks, slipping over the piles of bags and skirting around the large boxes overflowing with junk until … What is this? A pit. No, a staircase. But why? The long staircase seemingly descends into nothingness as Frank peers down the steep descent. How far down does it go?

A stale wind whooshes from the depths of the tunnel. Frank looks up, seeing the apartment building so close, just a block away. But if he goes back there, will anything really change? No. Tentatively, Frank begins the long descent into the void. As he walks his mind fills with blissful nothingness as he slowly descends the stairs. All that he needs to think about is where to place his foot. The reprieve from the mind games is so refreshing that Frank doesn't realize how deep he is until he finally turns to look back up the stairs.

As the sky above turns into a pinprick of blue, something hits him in the face. Stumbling on the stairs he squints into the darkness, waiting. How long he stands there waiting for something that is never coming, no one knows. Finally, he reaches one hand out and gropes the darkness, finally seizing a small cold chain. Slowly pulling the string, the staircase erupts in blinding light.

Blinking hard, Frank squints, looking around at his new surroundings. What is this place? Having been so careful to stay in the center of the staircase, Frank hadn't noticed the passages extending sporadically from the central line. Lit by the softly glowing bulbs Frank turns down what seems to be a street. Stores and houses lay abandoned. Perfectly preserved, it seems everyone had just left for vacation. Or maybe they're still here? Maybe they're just behind this corner. But as Frank rounds the side of the building, there is nothing but more streets and buildings under the low ceiling. Despite the lack of voices and eerie silence, something is there—he doesn't feel alone. Maybe a memory, haunting the forever-darkened streets that were once their home. Strolling down the streets, on a warm summer day with the heat reflected on the asphalt, burning toes, and sending everyone inside to cool off. How cold it is now. Years of darkness. Always wondering when the sun will rise but never given an answer. Where the sky once shone, there's a crisscrossing tapestry of pipes, looping behind houses, into shops, and disappearing into the rock above.

Frank follows the pipes. The streets are utterly barren, either scavenged or cleaned by someone. It seems as if someone will appear and start going about their day. Or maybe they're all just waiting to surprise him.

Whatever happened, it doesn't feel right. Why they left is a mystery. A mystery.

When every answer is available, every problem solved, the unknown becomes terrifying. For so long, we developed innate curiosity; maybe at one point it helped us, but now in place of wonder is fear, running down the winding streets. Frank panics. Suffocated by the memories, the lost sounds, forgotten voices, not wanting to know, not wanting to stay. Yearning for the surface, the bright blue shining gem that is the sky, and to leave the compressing, suffocating curiosity that has sprung deep inside him.

Legs aching and eyes watering, he reaches the surface. Panting and looking down the long staircase, fear and curiosity battle each other for supremacy. Frozen by the internal battle raging inside him, his breathing steadies, heart slows, and legs return to normal. The fluorescent bulbs call to him. The wavering, unsteady light exudes warmth and safety in the cold, curious, threatening world. The roots of curiosity have been planted. And like a weed, it will no longer be ignored. Once again, he starts the long descent down the staircase, into the unknown.

Chapter 32

REFUGE

ANOTHER. MORE. FURTHER. Now that he has given in, curiosity and fear work together to pull him deeper into the labyrinth of forgotten cities. But never reaching the bottom.

The days start to flick past again, faster and faster. First thing in the morning, he comes here and disappears until dark. Frank obsessively explores the streets with growing arrogance. Only two thoughts pass through his mind: he is the only one to have found this place, and he alone will discover all its secrets.

On each layer, something went wrong: a flood scars the building on one, and another is charred black, but most look as if the people willingly chose to leave. Support beams line the walls of each passage and solid concrete fills the space between layers. It looks like wherever a new style of building or a technological innovation became popular, another layer was built. Finally, rather than just building on top of itself, the city began cycles of rapid renovation.

But they didn't renovate the city. Not all of it anyway. They renovated the InnerCity, keeping it shiny and sparkling to draw the crowds, but they didn't bother to touch the OuterCity or the layers of the city that had been discarded. Everyone was more than happy to forget about the OuterCity as its shinier twin cast its shadow.

Descending the now familiar stairs, Franks halts and reaches for the cool chain dangling in the darkness. The warm metal falls into his hand. He pulls it. No one is there. Like always, no one else is here. But then why is it warm? Another battle wages inside as he waits, dumbfounded, for what to do next. What can he do? Is there really a choice? What if there is another person, who, like him had discovered these stairs? Perhaps they would have the answer as to what happened here. Down he goes, following the light, and watching apprehensively for anything out of the ordinary. But once again, nothing. No one looms from deep in a tunnel or jumps out behind him. Just stairs, and more stairs. Is this all he had been worried about?

The bottom of the staircase is just another passage, the last one. Maybe the answer to why everyone had forgotten this place is here, on this level. The streets, although much older than the ones at the surface, are littered with hanging pipes. A groaning, humming sound resonates from the walls as Frank walks down the streets. These pipes fuel the city, drawing the gas from even deeper than these streets to the surface to fuel the newest city.

The cement is cracked, and the buildings have spent so long away from the sun that everything is perfectly preserved. Was it real? Maybe he's just imagining this again. Frank stops and watches the scene trying to decide if he's imagining them out of desperation.

He steps back suddenly when, right in front of him, a tall blond girl appears with dark shadows under her green eyes. She absentmindedly strolls past him. She must be real. To be sure, Frank reaches out and taps her shoulder. Quickly stepping back, she looks at him carefully, deciding what to do. The next moment, a large leather bag meets Frank's face. He stumbles back, face stinging, but amazed. Satisfied, the girl continues on her way, checking to ensure Frank was not following.

She is real, and the longer he waits, the more people appear. Although few and far between, there are people here at this last level. A few peer at him through yellowing plastic windows, others look up from the cobbled road, caught off guard by the sound of the bag slapping Frank's face, just to be more disconcerted seeing a scraggly man gaping at them, wide-eyed. The group quickly thins as people disappear behind corners and into doors. In pure disbelief, Frank watches them leave until he is alone on the dimly lit street. They are here, almost a mile below the Zipers and skyscrapers. Far from the addictive lights and never-ending flurry, hidden in abandoned houses and streets, people have found refuge.

Chapter 33

MEMORABILIA

A SMALL BELL DINGS MUSICALLY as Frank tentatively opens an old door with an "open" sign hanging over it. The smell of wet carpet, old oranges, and dust rush to greet him. His muffled footsteps are swallowed by the store. Among the tall shelves are memories, scavenged goods that have presumably retained some value. Running his hand through a row of old jackets, a moth flutters from the folds and lazily flies towards the yellow humming light. The light entices the moth closer, to fly higher, and finally to touch it. With a soft thud, the moth falls to the carpeted floor.

Moving away from the jackets, Frank's eyes land on a wall covered in thin, different-colored rectangles. Next to the long rectangles is a tall set of shelves squeezed into the tight corner of the shop. Frank scans the shelves that reach to the gray ceiling finally landing on a label: "Memorabilia." The "memorabilia" seems to just be old advertisements hazily floating above their projection cores. Some display outdated watches or shoes, while others are invitations for a long past party. A birthday for a 5-year-old, a wedding. All forgotten memories are collected here.

But one is different; behind the newer cores floats something familiar. "Money reward!" floats in bold above a smaller message. "Volunteers needed for a low-risk experiment in the InnerCity. Come as you are! Help your fellow people progress into the future!" This is the same advertisement that landed him in this situation. How is it here? And why did whoever owns this shop think it was so important?

Frank walks up to the dusty desk and rings the small bell. The sound reverberates deep into the recesses of the shop, and, like a ghost, a small man appears behind the desk. His large eyes are gray, and they land on Frank, but he doesn't see it.

"Yes?" hisses the man tiredly, sounding like a deflating balloon.

Disconcertedly looking at the small man's furrowed brow and lined face, Frank says, "I would like to purchase this. Please."

The expression breaks and the man's demeanor shifts to one-half his age. "I'm sorry, nothing in here is for sale. However, I would be happy to tell you about the item! What are you interested in?"

"This advertisement please," he says motioning to the advertisement. The man looks at him quizzically before raising one eyebrow and pointing to his eyes. "What advertisement?" he asks dryly.

"Oh sorry, it says: 'Volunteers needed for a low-risk experiment in the InnerCity. Come as you are! Help your fellow people progress into the future!' Why do you have it?" Frank asks quickly.

"There are many things that I have for reasons I don't even know," says the old man smiling slightly.

"And is this one of those things that you don't know why you keep it?" Frank says, growing desperate.

"No," he says, smiling again.

"Then why do you have it?" he says exasperatedly.

The old man motions for Frank to pass him the flickering core, and he does. The man's fingers lightly brush over all parts of the small core and he begins to nod slowly.

"I have this because it made a friend very, very happy. And I keep it hidden because it now causes anguish. Put it back please, before they see," the man waves his hand in dismissal and turns back into the shop.

"Wait. Please tell me more."

"Like what?"

"Who wanted this? Why were they excited? Why does it cause anguish? Who brought it down here? And who gave it to you to keep? And what—"

"Listen boy." Frank hadn't been called that in a long time. "I am old and want to go to bed! All your questions will leave more in their place. I will let you ask one but pick fast," the man finished, crossing his arms. Frank opens his mouth, but then pauses and closes it again.

"Why do you keep it? If it causes anguish and hurt, why do you keep it?"

"I keep it because it once sparked joy. I like that it inspired joy, that it made someone happy. Even if it now makes them sad, the memory of that joy, no matter how tainted, is something I want to remember. And since I have no happy face to remember, I settle on holding the thing that sparked the joy. Just because something is tainted now, does not mean it loses its value then." The man finished and lets his words hang in the small room. Even the moths have stopped fluttering to listen. A moment later he turns and calls, "Now good night, Frank! And put it back where you found it!"

He disappears into the back of the shop. Frank returns the core to the back of the shelf and walks out the small door, leaving with a musical ringing. He was right, it did leave more questions than answers. One of these new questions is: how did the man know his name?

Chapter 34

MR. SPLIT

"FRANK?" A HIGH DRY VOICE calls to him from up the street. How does another person here know him? Whipping around, Frank looks into the street to see the woman from the furniture store standing with her hands on her hips on the small road.

"Hey… uh," Frank stammers, not remembering her name.

"Jes. Are you… ok?"

"I'm alright," says Frank, getting up and brushing off his clothing, eyeing the door behind him.

"So, didn't quite work out for ya, did it?" she says with a small laugh.

"Well, I guess that's quite obvious, isn't it?"

"So, how long have you been down here?"

"Just a day or so. And you?"

"About ten years."

"Ten years!"

"Don't say it like that! At first, I just wanted to get away from the InnerCity, but after a while, well, I have a real family down here. Everyone came down here for a similar reason, and we all stay for the same reason too. We don't want to live in the InnerCity, but we can't bring ourselves to go to the OuterCity. Most never even go up—too many stairs," she laughs.

"Ah yeah, that's the only reason," Frank nods knowingly.

"We have everything we need here. It's simple, but we don't want or need any of that fancy stuff. So how about you? Why did you come down here?"

She doesn't know. What if none of them know? "The InnerCity's waste became too much. So I left."

"Mhm." It wasn't good enough. "Well, we're all having a sort of get-together, will you come?"

"Uh, sure," he says, still watching the door he had just run out of.

"It's not like anyone is forcing you, Frank."

"I said I'll go," he replies, finally ripping his eyes off the door and looking at the bemused woman above him.

"Okay. Follow me."

Frank follows a few paces behind her as she navigates the labyrinth. The growling of the pipes is the only thing that changes as they move through the old streets. The longer they walk the more the pipes shake under the pressure.

Finally, she stops in front of a large green door. She knocks two times, then once, then three, the door swings open and a large group stares intently at the two in the doorway. The congregation is mostly younger people, but with a few older than himself. They all look happy, content. Although not in the nicest clothes or with the newest hair, they all smile as Frank stands awkwardly in the doorway.

"Everyone, this is Frank. Frank, everyone."

"Hi Frank," the group says in unison.

Clearing his throat, Frank croaks, "Hi," and waves awkwardly before dropping his hand in embarrassment and looking back to his shoes.

The group shuffles and forces Frank to look back up at them all … making space for him. Once everyone is settled, there is a space on the edge of a peeling leather couch. The large gray-green room is part of an old house; mismatched couches and chairs fill the dusty room. The wooden floors are scuffed by the movement of the furniture and groan under the shifting weight of the group. The same flickering yellow lights from the tunnels extend into the room and hum quietly in the silence. In one corner, the child from the platform sits with a small group. Exchanging the small pebbles he kicks off the train platform for other stones. The murmur of voices resumes as the group continues their conversations and those on the old leather couch turn to look at him. They all look puzzled but intrigued.

"So, Frank let us guess—OuterCity!" a squeaky kid pipes up from the other end of the couch. He blended in with his brown jacket so well that Frank hadn't noticed him.

"No way, look at that hair! Gotta be Inner," dissents a woman, after carefully looking him up and down over the rim of her large green glasses.

"Hmm, I don't think so—look at the dirt on his nose," another says, so close that Frank jumps, seeing a yellow toothy grin inches from his face. Scooting away, Frank rubs his nose embarrassingly.

"Other side," they all say. Frank rubs the other side of his nose.

"Sorry, we're being rude. It's just so rare that someone new comes down that it's exciting for all of us," says the man with yellow teeth, now retreating to a more normal distance, but close enough to smell, and see, the fish he had for dinner.

"Frank, right?" says a voice from behind him.

"Yeah," Frank says, trying to turn to look at who's talking, but the man hops over the back of the couch and lands squeezed between Frank and the woman with green glasses. Looking affronted at first, she snaps to look at the person who just landed next to her. Upon recognizing the man she smiles, losing all sense of hostility. He is disarming, with overwhelming confidence and a cheerful grin slapped on his face.

"Welcome! So, how did you find us?" the man says, adjusting to look at Frank and pushing back his frizzy blond hair.

"I was just walking between the buildings and found the staircase. I then spent a while going down the upper passages. I was honestly scared to see the bottom, but one day when I went to turn on the light, the chain was warm and I decided why not see if there were other people who didn't want to live in the InnerCity, like me."

"So, not a fan of the InnerCity then?" he says, stretching lazily.

"No."

"Matty. Nice to finally meet you!" He fervently shakes Frank's hand.

"You too. Wait—'finally'?"

"Come with me, Frank." Matty weaves through the couches, jumping over legs and ducking under the low ceiling until they reach the back of the room with a few cramped around a small table.

"Hey everyone, meet my friend Frank." Matty squeezes onto the bench around the table and motions for Frank to join him.

"So, 'Mr. Split', got tired of your second half?" says a man playfully to his right.

"Mr. Split?" Frank repeats, confused, turning to look at the man who has bright red hair and matching bushy brows.

"Yeah, ya know because you got split or doubled whatever they're calling it," clarifies the man.

"Oh, and that thing with the train too," another person with large brown ringlets adds.

Will he never outrun the other Frank? Does everyone know here too?

"Clever," Frank says unamused.

"Oh sorry, I didn't mean it like that. It's just we are all very interested in your unique position," the red-haired man says sympathetically.

The rest of the table turns and looks at the man with annoyance.

"What?" he says defensively crossing his arms and scrunching his doughy face.

Matty clears his throat before leaning forward and saying in a careful, but determined, voice, "We've been waiting for an opportunity like this for a while, so you must indulge our excitement, although childish," he says, taking on a winning smile at the end.

Frank doesn't say anything. Unshaken, Matty continues, "You know what it's like, the constant work—"

"The demand for excess," another says, leaning back in her chair, swinging her long braids.

"The insatiable thirst for things," another adds, shaking his bald head.

"They made it our burden to carry. But we don't deserve that!" Matty says. Around the table, everyone nods in agreement.

"We don't deserve to be treated so poorly, do we, Frank?" says the woman with the long dark braids.

"No?" Frank says uncertainly, and around the table, he's met with smiles and nods of encouragement.

"No, we don't deserve to be treated so poorly!" Frank says loudly, and they all shout in agreement.

"It's up to us to make a difference. To stick together! We've all seen the atrocities the InnerCity commits daily." Heads nod as Matty speaks, and Frank finds himself nodding as well. Matty is right, he has seen the atrocities the InnerCity commits.

"But we have also seen the apathy of the Outer-City." The table once again nods in sad agreement. "But we've broken through. We can see the problems in this city! And we need to fix them! Don't we, Frank?" asks Matty.

"Yes, but how are we going to do that?" Frank asks, enthusiastic but confused.

"What's the one thing they need, more than their new BlueScreens, trendy clothing, or Zipers?" Matty is looking at each person waiting for a response. Unsure of what to answer, everyone stays quiet. Frank thinks about the polka dots he had been forced to wear.

Slapping his fist to the table, Matty triumphantly announces: "Power!" Around the table, heads nod fervently.

"Power is what they want. Power is the only thing they really need. So that is exactly how we get to them!"

"But how? None of the officials have any power anymore. Even the governor is pretty useless," Frank tentatively asks.

"Ah, but not that type of power, Frank!" Matty says, shaking his shoulder gently. "Energy. Their precious TUs!"

Frank shifts uncomfortably, remembering how much he used to worry about his own TUs, and how much it had overcome him.

"That is what they value most. It is time for a new city. No Inner and Outer, but something that will work for everyone. No more waste, gluttony, or greed, but a city that works and moves as one!" The group calls out affirmations, and Matty allows it to continue for a moment before quieting them and leaning closer to the table. "But Frank, we need you to make this work. You're the only one who can show the InnerCity that we matter! The only one to tell them that we won't take their abuse any longer! That we also have power. What do you say, Frank? For the OuterCity, for your friends, for us?"

Caught up in the nodding heads and smiling faces, Frank does not hesitate: "I'm in."

Chapter 35

THE RIGHT SIDE OF HISTORY

"Come on, Frank. It's go time."

The entire room shifts watching the small group rise from the table and make their way to the door. Frank follows in their wake, and the rest of the room shifts back to their original positions. The door swings open and they pour onto the road, excitement tangible in the stale air. The pipes hum louder as if trying to squeeze the last moment out of their life before falling silent forever. The group laughs and shouts as they walk through the street, some complimenting Frank on his decision, others excitedly talking to one another about how everything is about to change.

"Hey Frank, good to see you're on the right side of history!" a tall man with a long beard says, patting Frank on the back.

"How do you know we're on the right side?"

"That's easy," the man says with a deep chuckle, "we're on the side of progress! We are looking toward a better future; we are working to unite the city. What is nobler than unity? Than equality? It doesn't matter the cost."

"But how do you know that this is the right way?"

"Because if it is the choice between suffering with our current world or fighting for a better one."

"And if we make things worse?"

"Then at least we tried," he says, with another wide smile. The man pats him on the back a second time.

Frank accepts the connection, and looks back at the man, "Matty sure seems on top of everything."

"Matty? He sure does! I'm not sure what he does during the day, but he always comes back with new information about procedures and experiments in the InnerCity. He's sneaky that one!" he finishes, and he must be smiling under the long beard because his eyes are all crinkled and squinty.

"But I don't understand why you would need a double person, instead of just doing it?" Frank asks.

The man chuckles again before regaining his composure and politely continuing, "Think about how the InnerCity arrests people. They rely on cameras and sometimes on DNA. If you're doubled, just split up. One creates the cover by being in a very public location while the other turns off the gas. If they watch from the cameras, they can't tell who's who, and even if they DNA or fingerprint test, they can never pin it on one person!"

"But wouldn't they just arrest both?" Frank asks, concerned.

"Ah, any lawyer hired with the thousands of TUs you receive can get you off easily! How can they prove that you, as opposed to the other you, did it? A fifty-fifty chance does not prove guilt beyond a reasonable doubt. It's brilliant! They don't have powerful security measures down here. It's almost like they want someone to try and turn it off. Then they remotely turn it back on and go arrest the person. Oh, that reminds me," he says, turning to look at Frank, "you still have that drawing of the remotely accessible switch, right?"

Frank nods and pulls from his jacket pocket a folded scrap of paper.

"Very good. You have to remember to smash it. Turn your back to the camera and hit it as hard as possible. There's a chance they won't realize it's missing and will just try to remotely turn it back on. None of them like coming down here. And anyway, if they try, we have ways to stop them—this is our turf. Ah sorry, Matty already told you all of this."

Frank nods again.

"Well, anyways, I'm just happy you made it all the way down!" he finishes, patting Frank's shoulder contently.

"Harvey! What are you tellin' old Frank?" says Matty, appearing from thin air.

"Oh, nothin'—just how glad we all are that he's here," Harvey says once again, smiling from under his thick beard.

"That we are! Now Frank, follow me over here." Matty leads Frank to the rocky wall and points to something in the tangle of pipes. "See here Frank, those red knobs mean it's moving gas up and away from the main source. Those are the ones we want to turn off. I know I've told you this about a hundred times," he says with a light laugh, "but, just remember to turn them to the right. The left opens the pipes and lets way more gas through. Whatever you do, do not turn any of them to the left."

"Why?"

"Well, if too much pressure is released, the pipes will burst, leaking gas through the entire city. Then it's just a matter of time until something sparks and sends the whole city up."

"Why don't they have anyone watching it?"

"Well, they did. But now they all just sit in their office up in the InnerCity and never come down here. I think they are scared too. We run the show here. All they do is occasionally look at the cameras to make sure it's still running, and even if someone turns it off, they just press a little button and turn the wheel back to open. But you are going to smash that. At most, they would track down the person from the cameras and arrest them just when they think they are safe."

"How do you all know so much about how they operate?"

Matty laughs and flashes a familiar bright white smile. "Well, a magician never reveals their secrets. But I am always friendly to particularly useful people. Ah, here we are!" He raises his voice to be heard by the rest of the group.

In front of them is a sparkling metal door with a single handle and bolts drilled into a large rock wall. It is one of the only new-looking things and it appears like a taunt from the world above. They are so confident that no one would even try, and why should they care with so many precautions in place? The group stops right before the door staring at it with disdain. How long have they waited to get someone into that room?

Frank awkwardly steps away from the group and towards the large rock wall. The shining metallic door looks like a blemish on its surface. The InnerCity has tarnished everything; even here deep, deep underground they leave their mark. Away from the heavy breathing of the group, the coldness of the cavern surrounds him. Unlike the tunnel under *Next*, it is dry. The rock that was carved away now forms a fine layer of sand that blankets the ground before the imposing door. Frank reaches out and grabs the icy handle before pulling as hard as he can. It opens like butter. Behind the door is a thin hall of flashing lights and cords. He looks back to the group for a final time. Met with reassuring nods, he takes the first steps into the hall.

Chapter 36

HANDLE WITH CARE

ALL AROUND HIM LIGHTS FLASH and rhythmic whirring sounds resonate in the thin passageway. Drilled into the ceiling are small cameras that rotate to follow Frank as he quickly moves through the hall.

Matty's voice replays in his ears. "You have to move fast through that first hall. It's going to be overwhelming and a little claustrophobic, but once you get past it, you can get to work."

He was right, it is claustrophobic. The passageway narrows so much that Frank turns and walks sideways, sucking in his stomach. The short passageway feels never-ending as he shuffles toward the opening.

Barley squeezing through the last part of the passageway, Frank emerges into a square room filled with dials and panels. It smells like a new train compartment here, he thinks, vaguely of chemicals and with the overwhelming smell of something pristine and untouched.

The mesmerizing blinking is distracting. Frank slows to watch them dance, but then Matty's voice replays in his head: "You're going to see a lot of dials and numbers flashing around in that room," he was right about that too, "but stay focused. Facing from the passageway look to your left. There should be a clear box over a large wheel, about the size of a plate." Frank turns and sees the very box in the left corner. "Walk up to it and remove the box. It doesn't matter what you do with that." Frank throws the box into the opposite wall. "Now you need to break the remote system. It will be on the wheel. Turn your body to block it from the view of the cameras, then smash it as hard as you can!"

He hits it with all his strength. The corner edge shoots pain into his left palm and up his arm. The small, shockingly blue box is more solid than Frank had anticipated. Cursing and holding his left hand in pain, Frank studies the small contraption. Unbelievable. At the base of the small box is a lever. Frank pulls it gently, and the box detaches from the wheel. A small light flashes: "Repairs needed, handle with care." How long had it been since someone replaced this, or even checked on it? It seems as if their backup plan was based on this machine working perfectly. Idiots. Frank tosses the small contraption into the same wall as the clear box. "Finally, turn the wheel hard to the right and keep turning until it reaches a block. You must not turn it to the left!"

The large, silver wheel beckons him closer, tempting him to try. Frank reaches out and grabs hold of the cold, slick metal and turns it as hard as possible. The wheel groans in protest, refusing to turn. But then, one pull after another, it slowly begins to move. Reluctantly at first, then getting faster, until on one final spin, the wheel suddenly stops. The pipes fall silent, and the hundreds of blinking lights flicker before dying.

The last gust escapes before the valve is sealed shut and the small room is utterly silent. Moments tick past, and outside, the waiting group listens to the enveloping silence before erupting into deafening cheers.

No more gas flows upward. It will be a while before this reality hits the InnerCity—the existing gas in the pipes will provide the illusion of normalcy until the miles of pipes run dry.

But change will happen.

Chapter 37

A FAVOR

THE CIRCULAR DOOR FLIES OPEN, slamming into the wall and knocking off a few pictures. The previously undisturbed apartment is just how he had left it before the experiments in the Otherworld, except for a mound of boxes.

Noting his entry, the room springs to life. Lights begin to glow, and a soft whirling sound signifies that the clear stairs in the corner of the room are rotating again. Quickly turning and fumbling with the lock, Frank pants while popping off his shoes. The door finally clicks as he kicks the shoes under the small table in the middle of the room. They are still perfectly visible, so Frank flattens and crawls under the table to grab the shoes. The fluffy white carpet burns his arms, and as he stands, Frank hits the edge of the table. Groaning and rubbing his head, Frank stands, slightly dizzy. The world fuzzes, and he holds his balance in the absurdly peaceful living room.

Here, standing is a man who looks as if he has been running for his life—which he has. All around him are cloud-like chromatic couches, a white fluffy carpet, and rainbow-shifting walls. But as this absurdity washes over Frank the fear smashes into him a second later and he is running up the revolving clear stairs, shoes in hand. Matty had said that if someone was going to investigate they would be watching his apartment and come when he got back. He can't show any traces of where he just was, and what he did.

Frank stumbles off the revolving stairs and hops into the bedroom. He flings open the drawer, rifling through its contents and grabbing two mismatched pieces. He's running out of time; they'll probably be here any second. Hopping out of the swampy pants, Frank changes into striped, black trousers and a khaki shirt, before stuffing the old clothing and the shoes down the building's garbage chute. For good measure, he grabs a jacket (if someone could even call it that because the sleeves are nothing but thin lace.)

Frank fumbles back down the stairs and throws himself onto the couch opening his BlueScreen and wiping his face of sweat. A knock on the door makes him freeze. They found him. Matty had promised they would never be able to tell. Wanting to ignore the pounding, Frank tries to turn his attention back to the BlueScreen. The pounding becomes more insistent. Frank quietly slides from the cloud-like sofa and loiters in the kitchen, hoping the person will just leave. But the pounding persists. Finally cracking the door open, the Franks stare at each other. Frank clears his throat before awkwardly asking, "Hey, Spencer told me to check if you were here so …"

"Yeah, I'm back, what is it?"

"Well, we're scheduled to meet with OOgreet, but I didn't know if you would be coming. You are coming, right?" I thought you might need a ride. So…"

"Yes, yes I'll go," Frank says, trying to look casual, but still breathing heavily. Matty had told him that he needed to find a good cover, and this is certainly something. "What's it for?" he asks, after a moment of thought.

"A sponsorship meeting for 'OOgreet'. Only one of the most important biggest companies in the Inner-City. They own, like everything," Frank explains.

Yeah, they do own everything, including you apparently, he thinks. But Frank doesn't say that. Instead, he says, "Oh yeah, now I remember."

"Ya know, I'm surprised you agreed. The only time I've seen you was when you were going into your apartment, but you haven't even been doing that for days."

"Yeah, well I figure this was important enough," Frank says, trying to smile convincingly. But lying to yourself is surprisingly difficult, as the other Frank looks at him harshly.

"Can I come in?" he asks, with mock innocence.

"What?" Frank says, turning white. He tries to hide his fear, but his palms grow slick as his mind races mapping the apartment, trying to think of anything that would signify where he just was. Finally, after the excruciating silence grows louder it snaps.

"So… can I come in?" the other Frank asks again, more pointedly. Nothing jumps out at him so, begrudgingly, Frank moves aside and allows Frank inside.

"Looks nice in here," he says awkwardly. The other Frank's eyes continue to scan the apartment. He can't know. He can't have been sent to look in his apartment, could he? The other looks back at him and sees his missed matched outfit.

"You're wearing that then?" he says carefully. Frank sniffs and nodes gruffly. He can't go upstairs or the other will follow and see the signs that he poorly hid.

"Are you ready?" the other Frank says with contained disapproval.

"Yeah."

"Great, follow me," the other Frank says as he walks to the balcony.

"Yeah, but what are you doing?"

"We're going out that way," he says, pointing at the small glass door and the open ledge beyond it. The other Frank confidently strolls to the door and twists the small handle. Retracting more noisily than Frank remembered, the doors open, releasing a gust of wind into the room. The wind flutters Frank's jacket. He watches in confusion as the other steps onto the ledge and leans forward, falling into the darkness. With a shout, Frank runs to the door. This can't happen, not like this. Frank stops at the small ledge looking down only to see the other Frank smiling from the hovering Ziper, just a few feet below the ledge.

"You were worried, admit it," he says with a smile.

"Was not. Now move over," Frank says stubbornly, as he starts to lower himself from the thin ledge onto the Ziper.

The cold air flies past him, and he begins to wish he had brought a jacket with real sleeves. As his foot lands on the blue surface it turns from light blue to a deeper, more opaque hue. His second foot lands on the Ziper and he stands, expecting to feel unsteady on the thin sheet—but it feels just as if he is standing on the solid ground hundreds of feet below. He carefully sits on the Ziper and it grows brighter.

It takes off, flying deep into the city so fast that he can only see the shifting light emanating from the plastic. It is fascinating; it's almost like sunlight through water or like the light that emanated from the glass bottle back in his house. His real house, not the fake. Do the lights still flow through the house every morning? Or have they stopped since no one is watching them? Shaking this from his mind, Frank looks up to see that he is being watched.

"Hey. Do you think you could do me a favor?"

He pauses before cautiously inquiring, "What's the favor?"

"I accidentally overbooked myself and need you to fill in for me."

Frank looks unsure.

"Please! Just this once, and I will never ask you for anything ever again!" He is so pathetic. The poor thing looks fried as he has become subject to the whims of the InnerCity. He's been so manipulated and used, and he doesn't even realize it.

"Fine, what is it?" Frank says, sighing. If he is with others, it's an even better cover and will help implicate the other Frank.

"You just need to go here and meet up with Nov, Daz, and Rain. I'll send the address over now."

"Nov, Daz, and Rain?"

"Yeah. What about it?" Frank says defensively.

"Oh, nothing."

They sit in awkward silence, neither knowing what to say and both unable to act distracted as the Ziper makes the rest of the world into a kaleidoscope of lights and the outline of shapes.

"Oh, and it's nice to see you making an effort, but just make sure to wear the outfits I bought you with Spence. They're more … me."

"Spence?" Frank says shocked.

"Oh, come on Frank, he's not that bad! While you've been gone, I've gotten to understand him better, and he's really not that bad. He was upset when you left, did you know that?"

"Yeah, I'm sure he was," Frank says scathingly.

He could never learn to understand Spencer. He is an uptight, obnoxious, sad excuse for a human, who is better off minding his own business. A quietness falls over the Ziper as they look at each other. If the other Frank can't see his side, maybe they're not the same anymore. Pretending to be the other Frank will be harder than he anticipated.

He had no idea the other had changed so much.

Chapter 38

BLUR

ACROSS REALITIES, FAR FROM the blue mist, far from Frank, the city changes.

Shrouded in its own sorrow, the city morns itself. But through the darkness, a new light emerges. Not the sun, but something brighter. The first rays of hope shine onto the city. Like the sunrise after a year-long night, this new light is perfect and pure. As light falls on the frigid city, it brings with it change.

In the night, a new group has formed. A few from the InnerCity, but most from the Outer. From the shadows, they have appeared, all insisting that their voices be heard. With the power gone, the lines are beginning to blur.

As the first light shines down on the city, they have a plan: they will get the power back. Somehow, they will rebuild. They have to. The city is gone for a reason; although cruel, it cannot have been purposeless.

Deep in the cavern, the show continues.

Chapter 39

LOSE 20 IN 20

THE FRANKS STAND ON OPPOSITE sides of the small emerald-green elevator as it shoots higher and higher, avoiding each other's eye contact at all costs. Frank watches the small numbers on the reader tick up as the elevator gains speed. 184 … 185 … 186 … finally slowing for 187 and stopping with a musical chime at 188.

"Welcome to the 188th floor," says a polite female voice. The two step out of the elevator into a large glass office with windows as tall as the ceiling and crisp white walls. A figure waits, silhouetted in the light streaming in from the window. As the Franks step into the room she turns, revealing a set of blinding white teeth. Taking long strides towards the two of them, she outstretches her hand and shakes both of theirs.

"Welcome Frank, and Frank. We are so happy to have you here. Take a seat!"

The two Franks look at one another and then follow the woman to the large desk in the center of the room where she motions them to sit in trendy, but profoundly uncomfortable, chairs. The discomfort is not assisted by the air conditioning that is cranked all the way up.

"Can I get you two anything? Water, tea, or maybe the new super-quencher? Here take one," she says, pushing two cups of bright red liquid across the white desk and eyeing them expectedly. Pulling the cups closer both smell the suspiciously gelatinous liquid. It smells vaguely of fruit, but the overpowering smell is meat. Both hesitantly lower the cups and look back at the smiling woman across the table.

"Oh, don't let the smell alarm you! It smells like meat because that's what's in it! A full meal in a cup!" She flashes a blinding smile at them for a second time.

"Why would anyone want that? No one is going to switch to a fully liquid diet," one Frank says.

"You're right, they wouldn't want to until they see these." With a flourish, the windows darken, and holograms appear projected from the white table, each with a catchy slogan: Lose 20 in 20 minutes, fastest meal ever, never eat unhealthy again, with videos of two of them holding the brightly colored drinks and nodding with fake smiles.

"When were these taken?" one asks confused.

"Oh, they weren't. We made them."

"How?" they both say.

"We can make anything. With your permission, we can launch this immediately! You two will be compensated accordingly, of course."

"It's definitely … something," Frank says, leaning back and tucking his knuckles into the pink pants the other Frank had forced him into this morning.

"Why do you want us?"

"Are you kidding? You two are the most exciting thing to happen in weeks! Anyone who is anybody knows what you two did, and watched the stream," she says laughing.

"We're in!" the other says confidently.

"Can we talk?" Frank mumbles.

"Please, go ahead. I know this is a big decision," says the promoter, sitting back in her chair confidently.

Frank gets up and is followed by himself into the corner of the massive room. There's nowhere else to go and the woman, although trying to hide it, is clearly listening closely.

"What is it?"

"First off you need to stop cutting me off. What I have to say is just as important as you. Secondly, we need to talk this over. Do we really want people buying these?"

"Yeah. I think they're cool."

"Why do you like it? It smells awful and probably tastes worse."

"So? We need the TUs. Especially you … remember?" the other Frank pokes his finger at Frank.

"I don't need it, and you still have plenty left."

"Okay, yes, but I want more. If we don't, someone else will. They can decide if they want to drink it or not."

"You need to learn the difference between wanting and needing something."

"Why does that matter?"

"Do you even remember when we used to work in the factories? The amount of time it took to make something and send it to the InnerCity, only to see it in trash bags and dumped in alleyways a few days later?"

"So? They're going to do that anyways, that's just the way things are."

"It doesn't have to be that way."

"Like we're going to change anything—give me a break."

"Let's just leave and think about it."

"You can. I'm staying." They look at each other in disbelief. How could so much have changed from when they were doubled? Why can't they see things the same way anymore? Frank looks at him resolutely. Deep in his eyes there is something unique, something twisted and strange. Looking back at the large holograms of himself, there is greed. An insatiable thirst for more. He wants more. He needs more. It is disgusting.

"I'll meet you back on the Ziper."

Chapter 40

HELL-HOLE

THE ZIPER SOARS THROUGH the sky, splitting the cool evening wind. They're going so fast that the wind feels like shards of glass against Frank's eyes as he tries to not let the other see his pain. Despite his best efforts, however, he does notice. The flashing lights and blurred sky settle as the Ziper slows and Frank quickly wipes his eyes of tears.

"Are you crying?"

"It's just the wind," Frank says, still wiping his face from tears.

"It—it looks like you're crying," the other Frank says with a small smile.

"Would that really be so bad? Feeling for once."

"What do you mean?"

"Aren't you tired of pretending?"

"I'm not the one pretending."

"You mean, you think this is you? The real you? That is the funniest thing I've heard all day," Frank says without smiling.

"It's not my fault that your life has been going downhill from that one decision."

"From which decision?"

"When you broke the contract."

"We didn't even know what we were signing! And that is not how this all started. I know you wanted to do the same, but you just weren't brave enough."

"No, I was smart enough to control myself! Smart enough to hold my tongue, smart enough to be successful even after you tried to mess it up for me, and smart enough to listen to Spencer, even if he was awful."

"You never even tried!"

"Yes I did, but you were fast asleep, and I was at the hell-hole of a shop! I realized that any embarrassment they inflicted upon me wouldn't matter if I still had the TUs. And that maybe there was something they knew that I couldn't figure out. And even if there's not, I realized trying to fight back wasn't worth it."

The Ziper falls quiet.

"The worst decision I made was not breaking the contract. It was volunteering for that experiment. Because that created you."

Chapter 41

BLAME GAME

"I CAN'T BELIEVE HIM! He is the most arrogant, selfish person I've ever had the displeasure of meeting! And he had the audacity to ask me for a favor! A favor! He wants me to be him! Like, take his place in an event or something because he messed up! And on top of that—"

"You should go."

Frank stops pacing and looks at Matty in shock and disbelief. Everyone in the grey-green room stares at Matty. He sits, leaning on a yellow armchair, still perfectly relaxed.

"And why would I do that?" Frank asks, putting his hands on his hips and leaning into Matty's face.

"Well Frank, as the gas in the pipes runs out, and no more flows up, someone will start playing the blame game. You should be with people who can vouch for your whereabouts. We're not very trusted by the government, and it'll be good to get some practice pretending to be the other because soon, your life will depend on it." He says all this with the most bored, tired expression. He even finishes with a yawn.

Frank freezes, unsure if he should trust his judgment. But maybe there is something Matty knows that he doesn't. And even if there isn't, he has to trust him.

"Fine."

Chapter 42

SLIPPING AWAY

Across realities, far from the blue mist, far from Frank, the city changes.

Like the faces of a coin, they can never see each other's side. The council does nothing but waste time arguing over every detail. The old division leaders decided that they had the same right to control the City as the newly elected council. They raise objections at every proposition for no other reason than to hear themselves speak. But the longer they wait to act, the further the people slip away from them.

Before, it was easy to tell who held prestige; it was easy to tell who they were supposed to be listening to. But now, the lines are blurred. Another group has risen to the occasion, a ragtag group intent on steering the world in a new direction. The OuterCity is gaining power. A power that is more important than TUs, more vital to life. They are searching for electricity.

Meanwhile, with every objection the old division leaders raise, they are losing the city's trust. When all you present are old arguments, you age with your thoughts.

Someone can only say so many things before their voice becomes nothing but a meaningless string of sounds.

Deep in the cavern, the show continues.

Chapter 43

FRANKIE

"FRANKIE" YELLS A WOMAN in a tall purple hat. "There you are!" She kisses him on both cheeks before hugging him. Holding his breath to not be suffocated by the lavender perfume, Frank puts on a flippant grin and tries not to recoil. Frank had tried to be as late as possible, hoping they would leave without him, but unfortunately, it seems as if they don't have much to do and were more than happy to wait for his arrival.

The roof of this building has been garishly decorated with glass flowers and rubbery trees that glow in the darkness. Small lights shoot through the garden, creating an almost peaceful ambiance, except for the deafening chatter from all sides. The longer he watches the tall fake trees, the more they pull him deeper. The branches of the trees shift in time to the music creating a hypnotic trance of light and sound and laughter. It feels more like a beautiful synthetic symphony than real life. He is brought plummeting back to reality as the attention of the party turns to him.

"You look phenomenal, Frankie!" says another who had snuck up behind him. He turns to see him smiling grandly and wobbling over to him in tall rhinestone-encrusted boots.

More people gather around Frank. They are dressed as flamboyant and fantastical as the trees and look as if they are also from a dream. Fabric billows in the wind that blows across the building. They all shout greetings and commend him on his fashion choice.

He wore the polka dots. He didn't have another option. They talk and talk, and Frank just stands there listening to their topic choices. The woman in purple, Rain, is very interested in tasting every hors d'oeuvre and drink at the party, and she regularly leaves the small group to snatch another off one of the large black trays that hover randomly throughout the party. When she returns, she quickly picks up her conversation wherever it had left off, occasionally bumping into the man with the tall shoes to see if he could maintain balance. This man is Daz, and he, although trying to talk to as many people as possible, is most focused on staying upright, much to the displeasure of Rain, who also seems to be pushing drinks on him. And at the center of it all is Nov. She seemingly runs everything, and although the party is for a man named Harpy, no one pays him any attention. She sits in one corner of the roof and people and drinks are brought to her. Harpy sits sadly in a corner, watching his party unfold while nursing a large glass of some brown sparkly liquid.

Suddenly remembering that he was supposed to be talking to these people, Frank musters the strength to put an outrageous amount of pep into his voice and he says, "Oh my, as do you, look at those shoes!" painfully smiling at Daz.

He doesn't notice his disgust at the rhinestone-laden monstrosities, and instead shrieks with excitement, "I know! I just got them 20 minutes ago!"

Grimacing internally, Frank gives him an awkward smile before turning and trying to walk away from the group. But the group seems more interested in where he is going than their own conversations. They all shuffle along as he walks forward. No matter what direction he goes, they follow him closely, eagerly asking him where he's going and what he's doing. He does his best to answer quickly and politely but they bombard him with more invitations and endless questions. No wonder the other Frank had messed up. No one, however, is more insistent than Nov.

"So Frankie, what are you up to after this?" she asks, leaning in so close he can smell the alcohol on her breath.

She smiles broadly and raises one eyebrow as he stammers, "Uh nothing, I don't think."

"Perfect. You're coming with me!" she says. It is less of an invitation and more of a demand. Frank shrugs and gives up trying to find an escape, resolving to watch his feet and answering the many questions that they throw at him.

"So Frank, what was it like in the Otherworld?" a young very pretty girl asks, holding on to his arm and fluttering her lashes.

"A lot like this," he grumbles, but when they all look up at him in confusion, he continues, "Well, the Otherworld is just so realistic, it felt like real life!" He slaps on a large flamboyant smile. It worked. The group all laughs uproariously. But they all stop as Nov approaches Frank and taps his shoulder.

"Well, this is a birthday party, but it's a bit dull. How would you like to hop off and go someplace else, Frankie?"

"Sure," Frank says. Immediately, the party shifts, instead of asking him invasive questions everyone wants to know where he is going.

"I don't know."

"Please Frankie, won't you tell me, old friend?" says a man with a green spiny coat.

"I don't know where we're going!" he repeats exasperatedly.

"Are we ready everyone?" says the man with sparkling shoes.

"Oh, we might meet a few along the way, but yes, ready?" Nov motions to one of the many Zipers hovering by the edge of the roof. Frank nods and the small group from a line onto the Ziper. Frank is last.

When it's his turn, his toes slowly inch toward the edge as the wind tries to push him back, telling him to stay. Stepping off the edge for a moment he floats, the wind rushing around and pushing him up onto the Ziper. Stumbling onto the smooth surface, he laughs falling into the glowing plastic. The others laugh with him, and for a moment Frank yearns for this life, to be wanted and sought by everyone, all clamoring for his attention.

"Frankie, you are too much," Nov yells, and he is forced back to reality. These people are not his friends. They didn't choose him. He doesn't belong here. But he could. They are so similar; would anyone really notice if he kept pretending to be Frankie? More people try to step up but are blocked by Daz and Rain, who purposefully place themselves on the edge closest to the rooftop deck. The blue plastic glows softly as the Ziper moves away from the deck.

"Alright Frankie, where shall we meet you?" shouts a woman, trying to sound calm, but the desperation in her voice grows with each word. Frank just shrugs his shoulders in response. Despite how desperate, how upset they are, it is fun in a twisted way, and as the Ziper pulls further away from the roof, Frank can't help but smile.

Without the protection of the plastic trees the wind grows to a deafening roar.

"Where to first?" Daz yells, but only her lips move.

"I am starving, can we go to that one new place?" shouts Rain directly into Frank's ear, patting her large stomach.

"I can't hear you Rain, speak up," Nov shouts back, but the wind is growing so loud only her lips move.

"Just lower the Ziper," Frank shouts.

"What?" mouths Nov.

"Lower the Ziper!" he yells again, this time pausing to breathe the thin air between each word.

The indistinguishable conversation continues until someone finally yells at the Ziper to go lower. Like a rock, it shoots straight down and the world blurs around as the bright lights of the city streak into long lines of color before finally the Ziper slams to a halt.

"What the hell was that?" Frank yells in shock.

"What do you mean, Frank? I thought that was your favorite feature."

"Not anymore apparently."

The woman in purple starts laughing. The Ziper erupts into fake high-pitched laughs before one finally asks, "So, where are we going?"

"That new restaurant."

"Which one?"

"With the lights in the deserts."

"Daz, honey, that doesn't narrow it down at all," laughs Nov once again. They all titter their high fake laughs before Daz finally remembers and announced, "I remember, it's called *That Table*."

"I remember, the one with the stage!" says Rain.

"Yes, so cool—and they just remodeled too!" Daz adds.

"Perfect!" Nov says and yells the name at the Ziper.

"Hold on, Frankie, this will be even faster." Frank grabs the bar just in time as it shoots like a rocket between two buildings. As the Ziper flies, reality melts away. All that matters is what they are about to do; all he has to care about is how he looks. The lights blur and shift, like synthetic versions of the colored light from his house. Mixing and intertwining in an almost identical way.

But just as the lights fade, a shadow passes over the city. For a moment, in the darkness, silence rings through the city, and nothing but the wind fills the growing void. The three others on the platform look down at the darkness in confusion and growing panic while Frank tries to conceal his smile. Like the wind, whispers grow. On the Ziper, back on the roof, and throughout the city, they grow. Whispers of fear, distrust, and panic now fuel the city. Slowly, lights quietly flicker back to life as the generators kick into gear, and the whispers begin to fade. But they will never die.

The generators will only prolong the inevitable silence to follow. The first spark has been lit, and the new heartbeat of the city grows stronger. Like the flap of a wing to a distant hurricane, the turning of a wheel is a spark to a pyre.

Chapter 44

MERCIFUL

ACROSS REALITIES, FAR FROM the blue mist, far from Frank, the city changes.

Change is upon them, and no matter how fervently they try to halt it, it has gained too much momentum. And that momentum may be the answer.

Pedals crank and crank, but the small energy is barely enough to flicker the small bulbs or push the dial. It's not enough. The Outers working alone cannot build the city back. They are forced to take action and fix a problem they didn't cause. It doesn't seem fair when none of them got to choose to begin the change. Even if they would have made the same decision, the option was ripped from them. One person made that choice for all of the city. One person who thought he knew what was best for all. One person who believed himself enlightened and more deserving than the rest of the city. He is mercifully exempt from witnessing the consequences of his actions.

Deep in the cavern, the show continues.

Chapter 45

FLICKER

"HERE WE ARE!" SAYS NOV, as the Ziper suddenly stops in front of a blue and yellow glass platform high in a building. Dozens of people mill on the wide walkway, occasionally disappearing into the brightly colored entrance. Holograms all flicker lightly, making the throngs of people look nervously around, concerned that their world is failing. A large image of a woman holding a shoe glitches before shutting off completely. In a single movement, people in dark clothing appear and replace the core with another, smaller one as people watch frightened.

This is not the InnerCity he left. It is now permanently changed. Faces look suspiciously at one another, and most continue walking faster down the bright orange iridescent walkway that wraps like a snake through several tall ornate glass buildings.

Back on the Ziper, no one mentions what just happened on the flight over. Instead, Daz weakly fills the air with, "They really need to work on the acceleration, the smaller models can go twice as fast."

"I know, it's so annoying. I have both, but mostly use this one with other people," Nov adds, desperate to prevent the silence from crawling back.

The platform shifts as they hop off gracefully. Frank stumbles onto the walkway, silently cursing the elongated studded shoes.

"Oh honey, are you okay?" Rain asks, grabbing his arm.

"Yes, the flight must have set me a little off balance." They all laugh loudly and carve a path through the people now hurriedly walking away from the platform. Unfazed, Frank's group bustles towards a blocky glowing sign with *That Table* written in orange. As they enter, red light radiates from the walls of the tin hall, and Nov and Daz try to squeeze through at the same time.

"After you," Frank says to Rain, watching Nov and Daz with amusement.

"Well, aren't you the cutest!" she says, going into the middle of the hall and waiting for the two to unblock the entryway. Finally bursting through into the restaurant, another high screech tells him that they had just found another person to entertain themselves with.

The small entrance into the restaurant is merely a distraction from the spectacle inside: the walls glow like embers plucked from a raging fire, flames lick high into the air from the kitchen, and a heater is on full blast. It is like stepping inside a living inferno.

A small group mills around one of the shining black tables shouting meaningless greetings at one another. From within the congregation bursts a man with gemstones for eyebrows with an orange-haired girl following shortly behind. The two screech to a halt before Frank and the man's thunderous voice booms in his ear.

"Hi there Frankie! Remember me?"

Frank looks at him blankly.

"Ray!" he says.

"Oh yes, yes, how could I forget!" Frank says with an awkward smile.

"Yes, well, I want you to meet my sister. Frank, this is Cay, Cay this is Frank—the doubled one!" he ends in a loud whisper. Cay and Ray, their parents were … creative.

"Nice to meet you. Would you all like to join our table? We can have them expand it," pipes the orange-haired girl, blushing profusely.

Frank nods politely and they all sit after another flurry of greeting ensues. A moment later more drinks arrive at the table and are emptied just as fast. Not paying attention to any of them, Frank picks up a small spoon and looks at his warped reflection on the surface. It has more lines and creases than he remembers. Still puzzling over how it seems years have passed in a matter of weeks, Frank is forced back into the conversation by the uncharacteristic silence.

The walls of the restaurant are flickering more than any flame. They are running out of power. They are running out of time. The walls go dark, and the only light is the tendrils of flame from the kitchen. Soon, even those dwindle out. Cay opens her BlueScreen to shine a light onto the table. The vibrant blue shines like fear in their eyes as they look at each other across the table.

"What do we do?" whispers Daz. Only the silence answers him as the group is at a loss. Finally, one voice rises. Nov says, "How about we find a new place? I'm sure they're just having technical issues here." She finishes with a tentative smile and the rest of the group quickly agrees with her.

They rise in silence. They are the last table to leave the restaurant, and their shuffling reverberates off the high ceilings. One thin hallway later and they stand on the empty, dark walkway, illuminated only by the hovering Ziper. Although it's almost the middle of the night, it's never been this empty. They stand in shock. Even Frank cranes his neck hoping to see any movement on the walkway, but nothing reveals itself.

Cay turns to him. "It'll turn back on soon. They just need to put in some new pipes, and everything will go back to how it was before. This is just an annoyance." It sounds like she is trying to calm herself more than him. But despite the reassurances, the city is darkening by the moment. Once a beacon of glory and prosperity, the InnerCity is now a fragile shell of itself.

They can't know what Frank did. No one can. Although Matty had assured him there was no way to catch him, he cannot make himself more of a suspect. So he says nothing.

"Well," Nov starts before lowering her tone to continue, "I say we fly into the Outer and, ya know, check things out." She winks at Frank as if he should know something. "I bet they have tons of energy and are just keeping it from us."

"Nov's right. They all spend their lives working in factories, so it's not surprising that they would be able to redirect the gas to only go to the OuterCity," Daz speculates, leaning in even closer. Frank can smell the stench of booze wafting from his breath as well.

"So what are you going to do?" Ray asks eagerly.

"Oh, just have a little fun," says Daz suspiciously.

"I'm sorry, what exactly are we going to do?" Frank asks.

"Little slow today, Frankie? We did it yesterday and you had a blast, remember?" Nov interjects patronizingly.

"O-Oh yes, of course, now I remember," Frank says and smiles weakly.

"I'll go!" says Cay, orange curls wiggling in anticipation.

"Let's get out of here. Whose Ziper?" asks the rhinestone man.

"Mine, we can take mine," offers Cay. "It's right over there!" She points to the only other Ziper hovering by the edge of the walkway.

"Daz and I will go grab the stuff, be right back!" Rain says with a smile, running back into the restaurant with Daz wobbling as fast as he can behind her.

"Great! Those Outers won't know what hit them. And this time, they really deserve it!" Nov says with a growing smile.

The small procession lines up, and each waits their turn to make the terrifying step over the abyss and onto safety. Remembering his fumble earlier, Frank jumps from the dark walkway and lands on the shining blue surface. The others quickly step on and the Ziper glows brightly in the darkness. A moment later Daz and Rain reappear both holding two large boxes. They pass the rattling boxes onto the platform before jumping on laughing.

Cay shouts, "OuterCity," and the Ziper shoots off through the darkness. Instead of the blaze of colors, dazzling lights, and music, there is only darkness and the whistling of the wind in his ears. The ride seems to last hours, as nothing moves below them in the city. Finally, the Ziper slows, and the two boxes are pulled from the edge and dumped into the Ziper. Large wine bottles tumble from the boxes making a deafening sound as they roll onto the platform.

Carefully choosing their empty bottles, the party sits back into the hard plastic, scanning the ground below. It doesn't register what they are doing until a bottle smashes into a window, shattering both and sending glass tinkling like gems to the concrete below and covering the black OuterCity street with a thousand shining jewels.

Frank opens his mouth to shout or cry, but the sound is overpowered by a flurry of more smashes. Someone yells from far below but the exact words are lost to the wind as they soar over the OuterCity for another pass.

More bottles are thrown off the Ziper, without a target they destroy everything they touch. Screams and crashes follow closely behind them as the "game" progresses. The party cheers and whoops as the pile slowly dwindles.

Frank is frozen. Didn't Nov say, "And this time, they really deserve it!" This time? They had done this before. He had done this before. Well, not him, but it could have been him.

Finally, the Ziper turns sharply and flies back to the InnerCity. They've finished their contest and are counting up scores. Reveling in the fun, the crew asks why he didn't join in this time.

Why didn't he? He's not "Frankie." He is not the person they think he is. But he wanted to be. That night, hadn't he wished that these were his friends? That this was his life? But he would never do this, he wasn't capable of doing this, at least he thought. None of them had realized they were different. Suddenly sick, Frank grasps the cold metal railing and leans over the side. The others watch him curiously. One slows the Ziper, and they wait for him to surface for air. When he finally does, he turns to stare at the group, wiping vomit from his mouth he says: "I'm done."

"But it's even 3, we can slow the Ziper if it's making you sick."

"It's not making me sick; you are."

Aghast and offended one says, "So suddenly you've grown a conscience for your OuterCity friends? We're not doing anything wrong. They asked for it! It's our power!"

"Yeah! They started it!" another shouts defensively.

Frank pauses, then speaks slowly, "It's not our fault you all have an insatiable thirst for things. You don't live, you don't think, all you do is demand more! And we satisfied that for so long; we worked, suffered, died, just so you could have new shoes and shirts, more food than you could ever eat, and more time than you know what to do with. But not anymore. You will never survive without us."

The Ziper sits in silence watching Frank breathing heavily.

"You're not Frankie."

"You're right, I'm not, and I am never going to be." With that, he jumps.

Screams ring out into the darkness, but no one looks over the edge. The Ziper simply disappears into the wavering lights and flickering screens of the Inner-City.

From the gravelly surface of a building ledge, a few feet from where the Ziper once was, Frank watches them disappear. He brushes the pebbles from his arm and shakily stands taking a last look at the InnerCity and the life he could have had, before climbing down the building and into the depths of the city.

Chapter 46

COLD CREATURES

"WHAT HAPPENED?"

"Some InnerCity animals were throwing bottles again and he got hit."

The small body lays in the oversized bed still with a scared look forever etched on his face.

"Did he have any family?"

"No. Well, I guess he must have but I don't know who or where they are. He came down about a year ago and since then he's never mentioned anyone."

"What now?" says Frank, tearing his eyes away from the gruesome scene.

"We keep waiting. We have to trust this will work. The generators are failing, and it's going according to plan," says Matty.

"This was according to the plan?" Frank says desperately. Matty looks at the others uncomfortably before responding.

"No, well, I knew there would be some ... uh, casualties when the power was cut. But we need to trust that the InnerCity will ask for help from the Outers, then it can be reunited. We just need to wait."

How long, minutes, hours? The guilt burrows deeper, infecting every piece of his mind. Was it him? No, it couldn't have been. He didn't throw any. Maybe it was another on that Ziper. Who had snuffed this life? No longer will the gentle thuds of pebbles resonate from the train platform. A few headlines no doubt, the news passed over a table at dinner or a memorial posted by strangers only to be forgotten like lingering smoke disappearing into the air. How many of us will be forgotten like this?

No, they are going to remember. He will be the spark to light the OuterCity. To make the cold creatures feel warmth. Once they see the fire, they will learn it is yet another thing they can't live without. When the ice melts rivers surge, when trees burn forests regrow, where there is destruction there is also renewal. Destruction is necessary, fundamental. Stability is fake, a brief respite between unstoppable change, inevitable chaos. The longer it takes, the more destructive the earthquake, larger the fire, faster the change. It's been too long, it's time for something big. Unity through destruction.

He walks alone back to the pipe-filled room. He is known, nobody stops him. The lights and whirling sounds are now silent, and the cameras are all dead. He squeezes through the passageway and returns to the square room filled with dials. It still smells like chemicals. Turn them all to the left, is all he thinks, in his pain and anger.

As he turns the large silver wheels the last of the gas, like a long-interned genie, rushes to escape its centuries-old captivity. A deafening sound roars through the pipes as they strain under immense pressure. He can hear hissing from above. It is time to accelerate change.

Chapter 47

INVITATION OF CHAOS

THE BEST DECISIONS CAN TAKE years, good decisions take months, bad decisions take minutes, and when fueled by anger and pain, horrible decisions take seconds. From the once ever-lit InnerCity, now in shadow, a new light emerges, a flickering, hungry light. Like so much tinder, the city erupts into flames.

Like moths to a light, people are drawn to the fire. They are fascinated by the possibility of their demise and the enchanting flickering of the light. All the dazzling signs and screens of the InnerCity will never compare to the draw of a flame, the invitation of chaos.

And as the darkness of the night is relit by the crawling creature, the abandoned factories are filled with hot, burned bodies. Fingers are pointed, but none at him. Why would someone from the OuterCity who lives in the InnerCity set both on fire? It's always the duality. InnerCity versus OuterCity. Isn't it just one city? Shouldn't it be? Was it ever? Maybe the city was always divided. Maybe it always will be.

No. The fire, although more destructive than anticipated, is a fresh opportunity to rebuild the city as one.

Chapter 48

ACROSS THE DARKNESS

ANOTHER SPARK IN THE DARKNESS. Not of a fire, but a thought. Across the city, two sparks light. It's almost poetic; one city torn apart by time; one person torn apart by the city. Across the distance, two want the same thing. Across the distance, two messages appear in the blue light:

You know where. —Frank

Chapter 49

A REASON

THE MOIST AIR IS HEAVY WITH the scent of mold and decay as the Franks descend the abandoned passage under the city. This time, however, the silence is deafening, only elevated by the steady drip of water. Without the music, without Spencer, or the BlueScreens, there's nothing to hide behind. There is a heaviness in the air, not from the water or the sheer weight of the rock above them but the mutual knowledge that they are no longer the same. When there is so much to say, sometimes it's better to say nothing.

After what seems like miles, the two finally emerge into the large room. It too is empty. From a secret experimental lab to a party hall and now to a desolate cavern. A few cords dangling from the ceiling and metal support beams are all that remain. The water continues to drip, methodically, determinedly. How many eons did it take for that dripping water to create such a place and how long was it until anyone noticed?

What are the odds that he could be here, now? But where is here? One small cavern among how many thousand? And that's just on this floating rock. In school, before the funding was cut and everyone had to switch to the factories, some teachers talked about the infinite expansiveness of our universe, something mere children were incapable of understanding because they could never fathom their insignificance. As children, we are willing to listen to others, we want to learn. Maybe if someone had explained this randomness to those children, now adults, they would understand their role in the world. That our lives are just an imperceptible blip in the uncaring, meaningless universe. Although maybe there's a reason that he's here, now. In one room, under one city, on one planet, in one solar system, in one galaxy, one supercluster, and one universe.

There must be a reason, there has to be. Why does he get to be here? Why do they get to be here? As if guided by a memory, they both start walking out of the room and down the long passageway, finally making it to the room where they first met. Where they first diverged. It just feels right.

Why did they pick us? Maybe he thinks the same. He's not sure anymore.

The other speaks. "I don't want to deal with this, with you. It's ridiculous. They think because you have my brain and body, we'll think the same?"

"It's not yours," Frank exhales.

"No? Then whose is it?"

"Neither of ours."

"It's mine."

Frank doesn't say anything and watches the other's trembling jowls.

"It's mine," he repeats louder. "It's mine!" He's shouting now. "It's mine! It's mine! It's—"

"It is not yours!" bursts Frank. "It's not mine either. Whoever decided to get doubled was not either of us, don't you understand? You have become shallow, frivolous, hedonistic, and an egotistical idiot."

"Shut up." Frank's face is flushed and getting redder by the second.

"Idiot," Frank whispers, and the corner of his mouth twitches.

"I said shut up!"

"Idiot," he again, louder this time.

"Well, if I'm an idiot, you are too!" he shouts, satisfied. Surely, Frank won't call himself an idiot.

"I am an idiot. I've always been an idiot. Do you want to know the difference between the two of us?"

They're so close now, staring at each other less than an inch apart.

"What?" he sputters, the sour word spoken so quietly and filled with malice that the air itself is poisoned.

Frank waits for the word to stop simmering in the air, before calmly saying, "I know who you are, but you don't know who I am. I am an idiot. I am shallow and egotistical and everything else, but the difference is this: I know I am."

"I don't know who you are, huh? I know you set the fire. I know you destroyed everything. You ruined everything! Don't pretend like you're all high and mighty, we've both done awful things."

"Maybe … But why did you throw those bottles? Was it to create unity? No. Was it to help someone else? No. Was it to do anything other than to have fun? No. That's the difference—at least I had a reason."

The other Frank starts laughing, coldly and sharply. "You—you think you lit that fire to help people? You think we're different? You think we've changed? We're more similar than either of us would like."

"No."

"No? How exactly are we so drastically different?"

"I watched you. I watched you get everything we ever wanted, and you liked that. I realized if I was getting everything, I would like it too. But I also watched you leave your life behind. You left everything. You became what we once hated. Maybe we are similar, but I would never have done that."

"I hate you."

"You hate yourself," Frank says, with a sad smile.

"You have no right to say those things about me."

"You're just a boy who throws bottles at windows and forgets his past, who forgets who we were."

"And who were we?" He is so close he could reach out and touch the almost perfect image of himself.

"We weren't anything. We were just a cog in a useless machine, and you still are. Do you know what happens when a cog breaks? It gets replaced. You are replaceable. No matter how hard you fight, you will be forgotten, you will be nothing! We are nothing!"

Frank screams. His fists and face grow hot, burning for action and across from him he sees the same fire building. Both yearning for action, needing to win, wanting the other gone.

Chapter 50

ONLY ONE

SOME CITIZENS ARE GATHERED in the street of what used to be the entrance to *Next: Medical Procedures and Cosmetic Alterations*. The fire has already ravaged this area of the city, and it is one of the only places that are safe from the tongues of flame. Red ash billows as a shadow appears from the mouth of the tunnel. In the morning light, the disturbed ash settles again as the world holds its breath waiting for a solution amid the chaos.

From the entrance there emerges one, not two. It is only one who leaves the tunnel, disheveled and shaken. One who quietly walks down the street, leaving the now yelling, screaming, fighting animals ablaze with hate and confusion. One who at long last pushes open the old, creaky door and makes the small spiders scurry away in fear. One who watches the sunrise and light pour through dusty glass bottles, dancing on the wall.

And one who cries.

Chapter 51

HYPOTHESIS

THIN WISPS OF BLUE SMOKE slowly materialize from the edges of his vision. The tendrils wrapped deep into his head gently pull him into the empty void between this reality and the next. His vision returns. A tangle of multicolored wires, a helmet locking him into place, and the small window with a face peering down at him, smiling broadly. Spencer, looking as punchable as ever.

Seeing that he is awake, Spencer smiles and gives Frank a small wave. Frank attempts to move, but his arms lay limply at his side no matter how hard he tries. The door of the pod begins to shake and groan as it slowly slides open. More faces look down at him now, some look saddened, others relieved. Spencer is the only one smiling.

"Lift him out of there!" Spencer commands the group. His ears feel like they've been stuffed with cotton and Spencer's grating voice sounds distant and muffled.

"Spencer, the experiment is over, you no longer have that power. Go sit down."

Frank tries to turn his head to look at the speaker but, again, nothing but his eyes move. The voice sounds so familiar, and by the moment, the sound is returning to his ears. Small clicking machines, a hum of mechanical fans, and loud rhythmic beeps. From the corner of his vision appears frizzy blond hair. A hand reaches up and smooths it back as the speaker continues, "Well, Spencer was right. Get him out of there."

Not wanting to believe it, Frank closes his eyes as many hands reach into the pod to pull him out. His eyes are still closed when they place him on a small, cold chair. They are still closed as someone sits opposite him.

"Frank?" the voice asks tiredly.

"Matty." At last, Frank opens his eyes to see the man he had trusted, leaning back in his silver chair with his legs crossed and carelessly holding a thin tablet. The clean white lab coat looks so wrong on him, but so do the bags under his eyes. However, he is still smiling, like always.

"You were a part of it this whole time?"

"Frank, I wasn't a part of it. It was me. This was my experiment. The completion of my hypothesis. And first off, I would like to thank you for being so cooperative." Matty says it all slowly, allowing ample time for his words to sink in and for Frank to fully understand the beauty of his plan. But even that slowly, Frank can't comprehend.

He stutters profusely, eventually, he asks, "What do you mean 'cooperative?' I didn't do what you wanted. I chose to leave the experiment. I ended it."

"Frank, once something like this starts, it can never end. Yes, you walked out on me, but that was planned. You even gave us a first-row look at the physical test. We got all of our intended results. You had to 'quit' and leave the experiment, that's what brought you down those stairs."

"There is no way you could have known I would walk down the streets or give up on the money."

"No, I always knew. My hypothesis was absolutely correct. I was able to correctly anticipate every decision you made—with the help of Spencer. That's why we hired him—he is so utterly annoying we knew he would make you want to give up everything, even the money."

Frank turns his neck to see Spencer opening his mouth, but then slowly closing it as Matty raises a hand to quiet him.

"And Spencer did his job perfectly, and I thank you for that, Spencer."

"All those people I met down there, they were all in on it too?"

"No. I was the only one, but they were all very willing to help me when I told them part of the plan."

"The shutdown of the gas?"

"More than that, Frank," Matty pulls his chair closer to Frank and leans so close that his lips brush his ear, making Frank flinch uncomfortably. He whispers, "So much more than that. They would never have agreed to burn down the city. They were blind, unlike us." Little droplets of spit fly into Frank's hair as Matty grows ecstatic at his genius. "Unity through destruction, Frank. Only we could see the path to unification. The smoldering bloody path. The path to beauty. The path to hope. The path to unity is through destruction."

"You can't have known I would decide to burn the city to create unity!" Frank whispers back, fear creeping into his voice.

"Can't I? That fire had been building inside you long before you showed up for my experiment. It had been building in you for a long time. All we did was ignite the pyre."

"So what even was the point of the pods, and the experiments there?"

"Well, that served multiple purposes. First, it got the government off our backs. They needed to think the experiment was legitimate. Second," Matty leans back looking shockingly composed and sane except for the glint deep in his eyes that Frank will never unsee. His brow furrows in a perfect imitation of pity before continuing just loud enough so everyone in the room can hear, but not too loud that his intentions become obvious. "We were confirming that you two were absolutely identical. If you are curious, you are—well, were. And last, it was very entertaining and got the city on our side. You demonstrated your violence for the whole city to watch in real-time, so when we had to nab you after the fire, they all believed you were facing consequences. That is also why we recorded your recall as well."

"So what are you going to do to me?"

"What do you think we should do?"

Frank opens his mouth to tell them to let him go, but he doesn't believe that he deserves freedom. Frank closes his mouth. The two stay silent as Frank works through what he deserves. He does not deserve to go free.

"I don't know."

"How about I ask you a few questions, and then you decide?" Matty says, and motions to another scientist. A camera is quickly placed before Frank. His hair is fixed, and someone wipes his face with a cloth.

"Why are you recording this?"

"Well, we are making a fascinating little documentary! We are going to edit me out of your recall, which we've recorded and then release it to the city along with this video. They will get their answers and we," he gestures to the others in white coats, "will disappear as normal citizens in the new city."

"But I—"

"That is not up for discussion. Ready for your questions?" Matty doesn't wait for an answer.

A small red light starts blinking, and Matty reads the first question from his tablet.

"Is it okay to lie to protect yourself?"

Of course it is, and Frank almost starts to say that before stopping. Is it? He had just told the truth, that he should not be set free. It would have made more sense for him to lie and say that he should go free, but he didn't. The silence in the small room grows thicker as Frank's mind races. All the times he did lie to protect himself, was it ever worth it? Does he deserve to make that decision? All the times he lied, did it ever help anyone but himself?

"No," Frank mumbles quietly, looking at his shoes.

"Is it okay to sacrifice a few to save the many?"

Again, Frank wants to say yes, that it was worth it, look at the city, working together, creating a better future for them all. But underneath it all is the haunting image of the small body laying limp. He should not have died for this. He didn't have to. His sacrifice … was truly a sacrifice. Frank looks up at Matty and sees him sad, for only the second time; his head is bowed, and his forehead crinkled. Matty thinks the correct answer is yes because he did make a sacrifice that should never have been made. He sacrificed that small kid for some idea of "unification." Was that worth it? No. But he made a worse decision: to set fire to the city. How many died then? More than one small boy. Was that *okay*? Despite what they believe, he no longer does. They were wrong. He should not get to sacrifice others for his cause. He should never have made that choice.

"No."

"Can we ever fundamentally change?" The other Frank certainly did. He would have never done the things the other Frank did. He would have never thrown those bottles or bought into the InnerCity. Or would he? When he was given the chance, he wanted to be a part of the InnerCity. He wanted to be wanted. To be a sought-after commodity, rare, valuable, and irreplaceable. For a short time, he was that person. And he wanted to stay there. If the other Frank had walked out of the experiment, would he have followed? No. He would have stayed and become the person he hated enough to kill. He is just as capable as being that person now. He is the person. The person happy to do terrible things to belong and be accepted. To hurt, to kill, to steal all hope. He chose to do those things. He was happy to do those things. Just like the other Frank had been. The other Frank threw a few bottles from a Ziper, he turned off the gas to the city, he left them scared and cold in the middle of the night to then turn around and set the blazing animal upon them. He did do worse. He tries to ignore the animalistic uproar inside him claiming that he is not the monster but the hero. He knows it is a lie. They are—were—the same. He still is the same monster. How can he have killed the better version of himself? And now... how can he live with himself now? Frank looks down at his hands. His knuckles are still spilt from throwing the first punch. Still raw from his betrayal. Still hot and burning for more action. But there is only one thing left to do. His punishment, the one he already infected on himself. The punishment he deemed worthy for himself. The only solution.

Death.

But how? Everyone has turned and is watching him as the small light blinks on and on. Finally, Frank sees it. Not a weapon, or a way to escape, but deep in Matty's eyes. He knows exactly what Frank is thinking. But he can do this, an apology of sorts. Frank looks into the shiny lens of the camera and sees himself; his scared eyes look at him the same way the other Frank looked before he died. But the fear of the unknown is nothing compared to the anguish of what he had done to himself. The prison of guilt traps him, and it is inescapable. Drawing in what he knows must be one of a limited number of breaths, he looks deep into the camera and says, "No, we can never fundamentally change … and I know what my punishment should be."

"And what is that?"

"I'm going to kill myself." His voice cracks as he quickly wipes tears from his eyes. He can't cry; he's done enough of that already.

Matty nods knowingly, and from his white lab coat he carefully pulls a small silver revolver and places it gently on the table. The metal is warm as he picks it up from the table and looks at the sleek surface. He toys with it for a moment, opening the spinning part and seeing it fully loaded. He won't miss. Frank puts his finger on the trigger, and behind him people shuffle as someone tries to turn away from what he is about to do. It feels hot in his hand like the metal is burning his skin. He has to act fast before he becomes too scared, or they take it away. Matty's hypothesis was extensive, but it did not account for Frank's realization that he was not the only person in that room who deserved to die.

3…

2…

1…

Frank points the gun at Matty and squeezes the trigger. The sound of the bullet firing echoes in the cave as Matty slumps in his chair. The room fills with screams. Frank's heart beats faster and louder as it works down its final seconds. He looks into the camera again, takes one last breath—it tastes wet and stale from being so far underground—and raises the gun to his temple.

"I'm sorry."

A LIGHT

"Do you hear that?"

"What, the wind? Yeah, I hear that every night while I'm trying to fall asleep."

"No, no, electricity!"

The small, disheveled group looks at the woman who suddenly stood from the dusty floor. She quickly makes her way through the piles of boxes and scraps to a low table in the middle of the room and begins drawing on the sheets of paper strewn across its scratched surface. She starts, and then pushes her wide brown wisps of hair over her shoulder so she can draw faster. They all watch her with a growing mix of concern and curiosity.

"What is this?" A tall man with broad shoulders and a shaved head stands in the left corner of the red tent. The few others turn to look at him, and as if on cue, the wind returns and buffets the tent's thin walls. They all pause to watch the support beams angrily rattle. After it passes and the tent is silent the tired group looks at one another anxiously.

A few step closer to the table and watch as the plan for a wind turbine slowly materializes. Seeing the amazement on their colleague's faces, they begin to crowd around the table.

She finally looks up, seeing the council gathered around her. They are the group taking action. They are Outers, and they are Inners. They are the council. They finally share one identity. They are finally working together.

"This is exactly what we have been looking for! We've all just been too focused on what might be beneath our feet to bother looking at the sky above. We can repurpose and modify the gas turbines and grid to work with wind!"

More progress is made in the next five hours than in the almost two weeks since Frank had disappeared. The heavy night air presses upon them, and the cold permeates through the tents and turns their breath into small clouds. Just outside the tent, a small tower is constructed from scraps, and the top blades of hope are carefully positioned at its pinnacle.

Large metal drums are pulled from the crumbled factories and carefully set ablaze to alleviate the darkness. The warmth fills the city—the dancing light looks so familiar and safe. But the crackling barrels are quickly extinguished as the night wears on. Not even the moon shines on the city tonight.

Whispers fly as they assemble the rest of the machine; they only fall silent when the wind does.

They wait for it to return. Nothing but empty silence fills the streets. Then it reclaims its dominion, as it always does.

From the small red tent, a light glows. They shout with excitement as the jerry-rigged turbine spins faster and faster as the gale returns with another gust. A light. A single spark in the dark.

And as that small bulb burns brighter, so does hope.

The End

Made in the USA
Middletown, DE
27 January 2023

23352303R00113